14.95

ALSO BY Graham Blackburn :

Illustrated Housebuilding

The Illustrated Encyclopedia of
Woodworking Handtools, Instruments
& Devices

Illustrated Basic Carpentry

The Postage Stamp Gazetteer

Illustrated Furniture Making

Illustrated Interior Carpentry

SWALLOW AT SEA

THE ILLUSTRATED ENCYCLOPEDIA OF

Ships Boats Vessels
and other water-borne Craft

COMPRISING

AN ALPHABETICAL DIRECTORY OF ALL TYPES OF CRAFT
PAST AND PRESENT CONTAINING MUCH DISCUSSION
OF THE DEVELOPMENT OF HULLS AND RIGGING
TOGETHER WITH MENTION OF SOME OF THE MOST
OUTSTANDING WARSHIPS AND COMMERCIAL VESSELS
SUPPLEMENTED BY A NAUTICAL GLOSSARY, BIBLIO-
GRAPHY AND INDEX

Written and Illustrated by

Graham Blackburn

Author of

THE ILLUSTRATED ENCYCLOPEDIA OF WOODWORKING
HANDTOOLS INSTRUMENTS & DEVICES

THE OVERLOOK PRESS
WOODSTOCK

First published in the United States of America in 1978 by
The Overlook Press
Lewis Hollow Road
Woodstock, New York 12498

Designed by Graham Blackburn
Printed in the United States of America

First Printing

LIBRARY OF CONGRESS CATALOGING IN PUBLICATION DATA

Blackburn, Graham, 1940-

The illustrated encyclopedia of ships, boats, vessels and other water-borne craft.

Bibliography: p.
Includes index.
1. Ships—History. I. Title.
VM15. B5 1978   387. 2'09   78-16565
ISBN 0-87951-082-X

The frontispiece SWALLOW AT SEA, from "Peter Duck" by Arthur Ransome, is reproduced by kind permission of Jonathan Cape Limited, London.

THIS BOOK IS DEDICATED TO

Arthur Ransome

who is responsible for
my lifelong affair with
boats

SWALLOWS · AND · AMAZONS · FOR · EVER !

Acknowledgements

There are many people whose influence and help deserve to be acknowledged. To all of them I am grateful but I would like especially to name the following: Henry Davies, who was there at the very beginning; the Walkers and the Blacketts; Commander P. Potash, Q.Y.C., Pacific Division, and Captain T. Holman, Q.Y.C., Atlantic Division; Lynda Redfield, surely the most beautiful of the Hudson River sailors, Brine and Wilf o' the Goats; and Maryjane, who does very well in the water without a boat.

To all the other people who have enlivened my existence during the writing of this book must also go many thanks, especially to Pat Sebastian, George James, Brock and Louise Brockenshaw, Christopher Day, Jack the Cat and Jubal, and most of all to Basia.

To the memory of Admiral Sir Cloudseley Shovell I offer my respects. I also like seagulls and am but a poor swimmer.

Contents

Illustrations

This is a list of those full page reproductions of old woodcuts and engravings not done by the Author.

There are few things in the world so
fascinating, so rewarding, or so productive
of the good in man as the art of sailing.

Peter Heaton, 1949

Introduction

Among my earliest memories is the fascination which things that floated held for me. Certainly my most treasured possession as a child was a wonderful model steamer which one actually fueled with methylated spirits to produce steam from its own tiny boiler and which would, after what always seemed hours of impatient waiting, move slowly out across the pond — one tragic day to sink like the Titanic in the very center.

The shock fortunately did not prove seriously damaging to my enthusiasm, and in the years that followed I filled the margins of many school notebooks with detailed drawings of innumerable craft both real and imagined.

The fascination has never left me, and this present book is but a more orderly extension of the habit, although I have the uneasy suspicion that it will not lay the compulsion to rest.

AIM : What I have endeavored to do is to present in alphabetical order an illustrated explanation of as many different types of craft as I could find.

While it is true that on occasion whales, dolphins, walnut shells, sieves, and even umbrellas have been used for water transport, I have restricted myself to more orthodox vessels; although such restrictions still embrace some very improbable means of transportation.

SLOOP

SCOPE : Absolute completeness, although probably impossible, would have dictated a work running to many volumes, so I have imposed certain limitations on my selection of entries. I have aimed at one representative of every known major type of vessel, from the earliest recorded examples to the most recent developments in nuclear-powered ships. What constitutes a major type is necessarily somewhat subjective since there is no ultimate authority, but I have tried to be fair.

It hardly needs to be pointed out that a separate volume might well be written about almost every single entry contained in this book, so it should be understood that each entry is basically an identification only, although often with some historical background, and where necessary a more detailed examination of important sub-types.

17 TH CENTURY MAST HEAD TRUCK

FORMAT : Even though related vessels, such as the many and various cargo ships, are grouped together, the entire contents are listed alphabetically. In this way it is possible to find any particular vessel under its own name; cross-references will lead you to its family if it is so grouped.

Since marine terminology has often been very confusing with regard to type names, I have chosen to group together only those vessels which share a common name, such as Dutch barge, hay barge, state barge, etc. This does not necessarily mean that all members of such a family need be related by either structure or purpose; it is often a nominal grouping only, for convenience's sake. Similarly, there are other vessels which might well have been grouped together by virtue of construction but which have been left separate. For example, the mumble-bee, although a trawler, is not listed under trawler since trawler is not a part of its name. (Being cutter-rigged it could also have been listed under cutter.)

BRIXHAM MUMBLE-BEE

Where a vessel is known by more than one name, both names will appear in their respective alphabetical order; the secondary name, after having been cross-referenced to the main name will appear in parentheses behind the main name, e.g. (**FREIGHTER** . see CARGO SHIP) will lead you to (**CARGO SHIP (FREIGHTER)**:)

Where a vessel is known by another name, often just a variant spelling or initials, which would be next in alphabetical order, it is not listed separately and cross-referenced to appear in parentheses behind the main name, but merely included with the main name, e.g. (**SAIC** or **SAIQUE**).

An entry followed by a colon (**CARGO SHIP:**) indicates that there is more than one type of cargo ship described, the rest following immediately in alphabetical order.

An entry preceded by a dash (**~ CONTAINER SHIP**) indicates that this vessel is part of a larger group.

An entry preceded by a dash AND followed by a colon (**~ GLOUCESTER FISHING SCHOONER :**) indicates that although Gloucester fishing schooners belong to the schooner family, of which they are a sub-type, they themselves have sub-types which are thus sub-sub-types of schooners, and which appear thus (**:~ FILE BOTTOM**)

Within each entry any vessel written in capital letters (... similar to a **SLOOP** ...) may be looked up as a separate entry. Any such vessel which is part of a larger group will have the name of the group under which it is to be found written in bold-face capital letters, e.g. (... similar to the FRIENDSHIP **SLOOP** ...).

Finally, all proper names of particular vessels mentioned in the text are written thus (**U.S.S. Nimitz**), and are listed in a separate index of named vessels so that they may be found again if you should forget what type of vessel they were mentioned under.

If this seems confusing remember that any and every vessel listed may be found simply by looking for it in alphabetical order. Major and minor omissions brought to my attention will be gratefully received.

At the end of the A - Z section there is a glossary of the various technical terms used in the text.

For those interested in pursuing further or in greater depth either the historical or constructional aspects of the vessels described in this book I have appended a bibliography of selected books.

HADLEY'S OCTANT

Graham Blackburn
CROWN & ANCHOR
WOODSTOCK
NEW YORK   1978

Types of Craft

THE MARINER   from DAS STÄNDEBUCH by JOST AMMAN, 1568

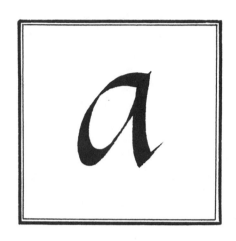

ADVICE BOAT   An Advice Boat was a small boat of no particular size or rig, but invariably the fastest available, used for carrying dispatches and orders to and from ships at sea during the period of the sailing navies.

AIRCRAFT CARRIER   The first Aircraft Carriers were simply floating hangars which transported seaplanes, lifting them in and out of the water with cranes.

H.M.S. Furious was the first ship to have a landing deck, but because of turbulence caused by her superstructure she was not as successful as H.M.S. Argus, which was fitted with a completely unobstructed flight deck in 1918 – the bridge being hydraulically raised and lowered and all smoke and gases being discharged over the stern.

In the U.S. Navy these vessels are called Attack Carriers, one of the largest of which is the U.S.S. Nimitz, commissioned in 1975. The **Nimitz** displaces **95,000** tons, is **1,100** ft (**335 m**) long, nuclear-powered, and with a crew of **5,700** can carry about **100** aircraft.

u.s.s. *Nimitz*

AMBATCHE   An Ambatche is a boat-like raft made of branches from the ambatche tree bound together and poled or paddled along on the White Nile. Like the **BALSA**, it may be the craft which has given its name to the tree.

AMERICA'S CUP YACHT. see YACHT, RACING

AMOY JUNK. see JUNK

AMPHIBIOUS VESSEL. see DUKW

ARENDAL YAWL. see YAWL

MEDIEVAL   ASTROLABE

ARGOSY   Argosy was the name commonly given to those trading **CARRACKS** (the largest ships of the Middle Ages), which sailed from the port of Ragusa, now known as Dubrovnik, in Yugoslavia. However, some people consider it may have to do with the **Argos**, the ship in which the Greek mythological hero, Jason, sailed in his quest for the golden fleece.

CARRACK

ARK   The Ark is the name given to the vessel said to have been constructed by Noah to save his family and representatives of each kind of animal from the great flood (Genesis chs. **6-9**).

The biblical account gives the measurements as **300** cubits long and **50** cubits broad, which translates into approximately **500' × 83'** (**152 m × 25 m**), and the material from which it was made as gopher wood. Gopher wood has been variously identified as cypress, cedar, and pine; it is interesting to know, however, that to this day people in the Euphrates-Tigris basin construct rafts of papyrus reeds which are called **GUFA**.

ARMED MERCHANT CRUISER or **A.M.C.** An A.M.C. is any **PASSENGER** SHIP or CARGO SHIP taken by the naval authorities in time of war and fitted with guns and used for naval purposes such as patrolling sea areas and assisting in the enforcement of blockades.

ATCHEEN. see BANTING

AUSTRALIAN GRAIN SHIP The Australian Grain Ships were steel sailing vessels, rigged as SHIPS or as BARQUES, used to carry cargoes of grain from Australia to England. A few were still in use up to the Second World War.

A STEEL-HULLED FOUR-MASTED BARQUE, TYPICAL OF THE GRAIN SHIPS

AUXILIARY Auxiliary is the term given to any sailing vessel that also has a motor or an engine. This definition now includes the majority of CRUISING YACHTS, and in America, by U.S. Coast Guard regulation, all commercial sailing vessels.

THE FISHERMAN   from DAS STÄNDEBUCH by JOST AMMAN, 1568

BAHAMA DINGHY . see DINGHY

BAJAK   A Bajak is a lugsail-rigged sailing boat used by
                the Dyaks of Borneo, Sumatra, and the Celebes.
The hull averaged **40'** (**12m**) long, although a large square
stern rested on, and overhung, the hull.

BALANCELLE. see NAVICELLO

BALD-HEADED SCHOONER. see SCHOONER, RAM

BALDIE   The name Baldie is a contraction of Garibaldi, by which this vessel was originally known in Aberdeenshire. It is a double-ended fishing boat, similar to a FIFIE, used off the east coast of Scotland all the way from Aberdeen to Fife. Lugsail-rigged, often with a mizzen which trimmed to a boomkin, and a jib which trimmed to a long bowsprit, it was from 25' (7.6 m) on the keel and upward.

BALINGER or **BALLINGER**   The Balinger was a small, seagoing vessel used in the Middle Ages for coastal trade, and sometimes as a TRANSPORT SHIP carrying about 40 soldiers.

BALSA   The Balsa was originally a raft used for fishing off the west coast of South America. The raft has given its name to the extremely light wood from which it is made. Balsa wood was used for Thor Heyerdahl's raft **Kon-Tiki** on which he and five others drifted 3,800 miles (6,080 km) from Peru to Polynesia in 1947.

The Indians on Lake Titicaca between Peru and Bolivia made sailing Balsas out of reeds lashed together.

BALTIC DANDY. see DANDY

BALTIC SLOOP. see SLOOP

BALTIMORE CLIPPER. see CLIPPER

BANCA. see CANOE

BANG CHOON   A Bang Choon is a net boat used in
the Singapore fisheries. Averaging
35' - 40' (10m-12m) in length, the hull is built with considerable sheer, the keel running parallel to the gunwale, so
that when unladen the forefoot and heel are both above
water.

HEEL   FOREFOOT

BANGKOK SAMPAN. see SAMPAN

WHALING HARPOON

BANKER

A Banker is a large fishing vessel that works the offshore fishing banks of the North Atlantic. Bankers were previously **SCHOONERS** of the **GLOUCESTER FISHING SCHOONER** type, but have now been replaced by modern motor vessels of the type illustrated below. They average **1,000** tons, **200'** (**60m**) in length, and carry up to **50** DORIES and **70** crew.

DORIES —

BANKFISKERSKOÏTE

Also called a Bankskoïte, this was the Norwegian sailing boat that fished for cod off the west coast of Norway before the motor-driven vessels.

← 60' (18m) →

BANTING (ATCHEEN)

The Banting is a fast sailing **DUGOUT** from Johore, one of the states of Malaysia. The hull is so carved as to have a clipper-type bow and a keel. The rig consists of two balance lugsails, and a jib carried to a short bowsprit.

CLIPPER BOW

30' (9m)

BARCA - LONGA

Sometimes spelled Barqua-longa or Barcolongo, the word Barca-longa comes from the Italian word meaning **SKIFF** or **BARGE**. It referred to a large Spanish fishing boat used from the 17th to 19th centuries. The boats were about 70' (21.3 m) long, and carried two or three single lugsails.

BARGE:

Barge probably comes from the Latin word "barca," which makes it the equivalent of **BARQUE** or **BARK**. However, today not only do **BARQUE** and Barge have different meanings, but Barge itself has several definitions, as listed on the next page.

a. The oldest use of the word Barge was for a small sea-going ship, the next size above a BALINGER. From the 17th century on, such sailing ships were called BARQUES.

b. A Barge may also be a ceremonial vessel of state; see STATE BARGE on the following page.

c. The third meaning of Barge is as a coastal trading vessel of the THAMES BARGE type.

d. The hull of a Barge of type **c.** above when towed by a tug and without any means of self-propulsion is known usually as a Dumb Barge, but is more properly called a LIGHTER.

e. In the sailing days of the British Navy a Barge was the second boat of a WARSHIP, pulled by fourteen oars and used for carrying officers from ship to shore. An Admiral's Barge, however, descends from the STATE BARGE, and was at first a small steamboat, but now is a MOTOR BOAT used for the harbor transport of flag officers.

f. A final definition of Barge is the now obsolete double-decked vessel which was used for carrying passengers and freight, and which was always towed behind a STEAM BOAT.

~ **DUTCH BARGE** The so-called Dutch Barge was in fact merely an older type of THAMES BARGE distinguished by its flat, overhanging bow.

DUTCH BOW →   OLD TYPE
1825

NEW TYPE
1925

~ HAY BARGE

A Hay Barge was a THAMES BARGE-type with a shallower draft for entering narrow inlets on the English east coast. To accommodate the high stacks of hay carried, the mainsail had a very high foot, and the helmsman took orders from a man conning the vessel from high on the stack.

~ STATE BARGE

A state Barge is usually richly ornamented and propelled by oars, such as Cleopatra's Barge which was "like a burnished throne" with purple sails and silver oars.

AFTER AN ETCHING OF THE STATE BARGE OF THE STATIONER'S COMPANY
BY E.W. COOKE, 1829

33

~ THAMES BARGE

The Thames Barge is a large, flat-bottomed boat with leeboards instead of a keel so that it may operate to windward in shoal water and remain upright if grounded. They are usually ketch- or yawl-rigged with a large main spritsail and a very small mizzen. The mast is normally stepped in a lutchet, which enables it to be lowered when passing under bridges.

SPRIT

SPRITSAIL

MIZZEN

SAILS USUALLY STAINED WITH RED OCHRE AND OIL

LEEBOARD

~ TOPSAIL BARGE

The Topsail Barge is basically a THAMES BARGE with a slightly different rig, better adapted for sea than river sailing.

BARKENTINE . see BARQUENTINE

BARQUE or **BARK**   The term Barque (usually spelled Bark in America) comes originally from the Latin, 'barca', and over the years has had different meanings as follows.

a.   Originally, Barque was a general term to describe any small sailing ship of any rig. See also BARGE.

b.   By the Middle Ages the term had become somewhat more closely defined and referred to small Mediterranean craft with combinations of square, lateen, and fore-and-aft sails. There were, however, many varieties, of which the illustration below is but one example.

THREE-MASTED MEDITERRANEAN BARQUE

c.   Small English ships in the **18**th century with no mizzen topsail were commonly called Barques.

d.   In America, however, Barque did not refer to a type of rigging as at **c.** above, but to a type of square-sterned and flush-decked hull, the majority of which were BRIGANTINES.

c.   After the middle of the 19th century the word Barque meant a ship with at least three masts, all square-rigged except the aftermost one which was fore-and-aft rigged. Also, from this point on the size of these vessels increased greatly from relatively small ships to the huge 5,000 ton five-masters used in the South American grain and nitrate trade.

A few small Barques are still used for inter-island Pacific trading, and as charter boats for pleasure cruises. Several of the larger ones are still in commission as TRAINING SHIPS.

THREE-MASTED BARQUE

FOUR-MASTED BARQUE
(SEE ALSO AUSTRALIAN GRAIN SHIP)

FIVE-MASTED STEEL BARQUE

BARQUENTINE (BARKENTINE): In the same way that the ordinary BARQUE, as illustrated on the previous page, may be thought of as the ship rig of the 16th century brought up to date, so may the modern Barquentine be thought of as a modernized revival of the 16th century CARAVEL. However, although the development of the BARQUE may be traced fairly continuously from early times on, the Barkentine as such was not known before 1830. It may be characterized as a sailing vessel of at least three masts, only the forward of which is square-rigged, the remainder being fore-and-aft rigged.

SIXTEENTH CENTURY SHIP
AND
MODERN BARQUE

SIXTEENTH CENTURY CARAVEL
AND
MODERN BARQUENTINE

FOUR-MASTED BARQUENTINE

FIVE-MASTED BARQUENTINE

SIX-MASTED BARQUENTINE

~ JACKASS-BARQUE

It sometimes occurred that a ship was rigged with square sails on the top and top-gallant mainmast but with a fore-and-aft sail on the lower mainmast. This partial transformation of a **BARQUE** into a Barquentine was known as a Jackass-Barque, although in England the term Jackass-Barque seems to have been reserved for four-masted ships, the two forward of which were square-rigged, and the two aft being fore-and-aft rigged.

It may be argued that Jackass-Barques (by virtue of their name) belong more properly with **BARQUES** than with Barquentines, but nautical terminology has always been notoriously confusing, and the fact is that a Jackass-Barque is merely a less-advanced stage of Barquentine. As competition from **STEAMSHIPS** increased, there was an effort to reduce costs on sailing ships, and one way to do this was by reducing crew. Since square-riggers required more crew than fore-and-aft rigged boats, the change was inevitable.

MAIN MAST

THREE-MASTED JACKASS-BARQUE

FOUR-MASTED JACKASS-BARQUE

BARQUETTE

A Barquette is a lugsail-rigged boat, around **20'** (**6m.**) long that was once common off the French and Spanish Riviera, very similar to the Madeira and Portuguese fishing boats.

ROUNDED STERN — HIGH STEM

BARRICADO

A Barricado was a small all-purpose boat attending **WARSHIPS** in harbor during the **16**th century. It usually belonged to the dockyard and was manned by civilians, although the term is naval.

BATEAU

Originally a French word meaning no more than boat, Bateau, by the early **18**th century referred to the double-ended, flat-bottomed boat much used by the French-Canadians on the Great Lakes and St. Lawrence River.

END VIEW

BATEELE .   see DHOW

BATELO .   see DHOW

BATELOE   The Bateloe is the large and strong wooden boat used to carry rubber on the River Madeira in Brazil, from Bolivia to the Amazon. The river is only **250 m (400 km)** long but has nineteen dangerous cataracts, and so many men die of fever, that it is known as the "Long Cemetery".

BATHYSCAPHE   The Bathyscaphe, developed by Auguste Piccard, is a navigable diving vessel. Several models have been built, the most successful having dived **35, 810' (10,916 m.)** in the Pacific Mariana Trench.

THE FIRST
BATHYSCAPHE,
BUILT 1946-1948

FNRS 2

FLOAT FILLED WITH GASOLINE

OBSERVER'S CABIN

BATHYSPHERE

The Bathysphere is a spherical steel vessel suspended by a cable from a surface vessel. It is fitted with portholes for undersea observation and made its first dive in **1930**. It ultimately reached a depth of **3,000'** (**900 m.**) but was supplanted by the safer **BATHYSCAPHE** since the risk of the cable breaking, which would have meant certain death for the occupants, was too great.

SUSPENSION CABLE

NEW YORK ZOOLOGICAL SOCIETY BATHYSPHERE

BATHYSPHERE , BUILT BY WILLIAM BEEBE & OTIS BARTON

BATTLE-CRUISER

Battle-cruisers were first developed in Britain by Admiral Sir John Fisher as advance scouts of the battle fleet. They were similar to **BATTLESHIPS** but with thinner armour so they could go faster.

13½" GUNS
SPEED: 28 KNOTS

H.M.S. Lion
BUILT: 1910

BATTLESHIP :

The Battleship is a direct descendant of the SHIP-OF-THE-LINE (of battle), see under WARSHIPS. The transition began around 1860 when iron plates began to cover the sides of wooden vessels, and steam propulsion began to be used. The transition was gradual, however, and for a long time these ships were known first as IRONCLADS and then as MASTLESS SHIPS.

The first true Battleship, completely armoured, driven by machinery, and having all big guns, was H.M.S. DREADNOUGHT, introduced by Admiral Sir John Fisher in 1906. This ship so completely revolutionized Battleship design that every other major power began building its own DREADNOUGHTS, as the class was known for the next forty years.

Air power has almost rendered Battleships obsolete (the Royal Navy scrapped her Battleship, H.M.S. Vanguard, in 1960), although U.S.S. New Jersey was successfully used for bombardment off Vietnam in 1968.

THE LAST, AND BIGGEST, BRITISH BATTLESHIP, H.M.S. Vanguard

COST (EXCLUDING LARGE GUNS INHERITED FROM OLDER SHIPS):
£9,000,000 , $35,000,000 , 1946

43

~ POCKET BATTLESHIP

The Treaty of Versailles limited the size of German Battleships to **10,000** tons and so three of these Pocket Battleships were built between **1930** and **1940**. They were armed like Battleships but had diesel propulsions which gave them a very long range so they were used for commerce destruction.

11" (279 mm) GUNS
SPEED: 26 KNOTS

GERMAN POCKET BATTLESHIP Admiral Scheer

BAURUA.   see PROA

BAWLEY   A Bawley is a small coastal fishing vessel used for shrimping or oyster dredging in the Thames Estuary.   They are now largely replaced by motorized vessels.

LOOSE-FOOTED MAINSAIL
(NO BOOM)

VERTICAL STEM
LONG BOWSPRIT

← 25' (7 m) →

BELGIAN LUGGER . see LUGGER

BELLUM A Bellum is a long, CANOE-shaped boat used in Iraq. It is paddled or poled, if the water is not too deep. The larger ones can carry up to **25** men.

BERGANTINA The Bergantina was the **15**th century Mediterranean counterpart of the English PINNACE — a small rowing or sailing vessel often carried (as by Columbus) 'knocked-down' in the holds of ships for assembly at any coast that could provide suitable wood for planking.

BERMUDA SLOOP . see SLOOP

BERTHON BOAT Invented by Edward Berthon (**1813** to **1899**), the Berthon Boat was a collapsible LIFEBOAT much used on DESTROYERS and SUBMARINES because when folded they could be stowed in a small space.

BEZAN (BIZAN) This word comes from the Dutch, 'bezaan,' and referred to a small 17th century KETCH-rigged YACHT.

BILANCELLA . see NAVICELLO

BELAYED TO A BOLLARD

BILANDER or BILLANDER

The Bilander was a small European merchant ship of the 17th and 18th centuries sometimes used in the North Sea but usually confined to the Mediterranean. Its distinguishing feature was the cut-off lateen sail on the mainmast, the foremast being square-rigged.

LATEEN SAIL CUT-OFF

BILLY-BOY or BILLY-BOAT

The Billy-boy was a river BARGE type of coasting vessel, originating in Holland but used extensively off the east coast of England around Yorkshire until the beginning of the 20th century. Late models were KETCH-rigged.

LEEBOARD

BINABINA   A Binabina is a CANOE from the Solomon Islands, similar to the MON.

STERN →   BOW ←

HAWSER BENDS

BIREME   A Bireme is a GALLEY that has two banks of oars. Sails were used when there was a favorable wind, but for the most part, and especially when fighting, oars were relied on.

Biremes were used by the Assyrians (700 B.C.), Phoenecians, Greeks, and Romans and others in the Mediterranean, until the mid- 17th century.

GREEK BIREME, O B.C.

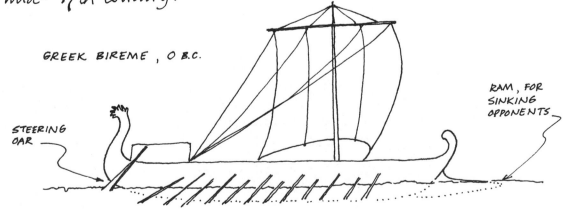

RAM, FOR SINKING OPPONENTS

STEERING OAR

BISQUINE   A Bisquine is a two-masted, lugsail-rigged fishing boat of around **40'** (12m) long, used off St. Malo, France.

LUG TOPSAILS

LONG, OVERHANGING COUNTER

VERTICAL STEM

BIZAN.   see BEZAN

BLACKBALLER   Blackballers were PACKET ships belonging either to the New York company of Marshall & Co., or the English company known as the Australian Black Ball Line, both companies flying flags bearing a black ball.

BLACK SHIP   A ship built of teak in India, during the days of sail, was known by British shipbuilders as a Black ship, presumably refering to the men who built the ship rather than to the teak, which is as pale as oak.

BLACKWALL FRIGATE. see FRIGATE

BLOCK ISLAND BOAT A Block Island Boat is a kind of CAT SCHOONER, sharp-ended and open, built with a keel. The forward sail is loose-footed; both sails have narrow heads. So called because it was common at Block Island, Rhode Island.

NARROW HEAD

NO BOOM ON FORESAIL

BLOCKSHIP A Blockship may be any vessel, usually one that is obsolete, which is sunk in such a position as to block an entrance to a port or a channel in wartime, or occasionally to fill a gap in a breakwater.

BOAT To the seaman a Boat is quite distinct from a SHIP, being generally a small, open craft, with no decking, rowed or with a small sail. However, there are some exceptions to this general definition, such as fishing boats and SUBMARINES, which were originally called submarine boats. People ashore often say Boat when they really mean SHIP, as, for example, do railroad companies when they refer to BOAT TRAINS and MAIL BOATS.

BOEIER

The Boeier is a Dutch boat that originated in the 16th century as a fairly large (65' (20m)) seagoing merchant vessel. By the 19th century it had become rather smaller, the rig had changed, and it was used principally on inland waterways with a single mast stepped in a tabernacle so that it could be lowered when passing under bridges.

BOEIER 1560

BOEIER 1900

BOMBARDA   A Bombarda was an Italian form of
                     BRIGANTINE with masts made from
single poles (like a POLACRE) instead of in sections.

POLE MAST

SQUARE SAILS FURLED

BOMB KETCH. see KETCH

BOMBSCHUITE   The Bombschuite is a decked, tub-
                        shaped Dutch fishing boat, remarkable
for its unique YAWL rig.

LEEBOARD

BOOM BOAT

Of the various small boats a ship carries on board, the smaller ones usually hang in davits along the side, the larger ones, called Boom boats are stowed amidships between the fore- and mainmasts.

BORNHOLM HERRING BOAT

Bornholm Herring Boats, from the island of Bornholm in the Baltic Sea, are Danish DANDY-rigged fishing boats about 22' (6m) long.

BOTTER

The Botter is one of the best Dutch sea YACHTS. It has a rounded bow and a pointed stern; a flat-bottomed, curved-side boat, it has leeboards.

BOULOGNE DRIFTER.   see DRIFTER

BOVO   The Bovo is a two-masted, lateen-rigged fishing vessel which worked the Gulf of Genoa, Italy.

BRAGAGNA   The Bragagna, which is very similar to the FELUCCA, is a three-masted, lateen-rigged boat which came from Dalmatia and was very common in the Adriatic up to the 1850's.

BRAGOZZI

A Bragozzi is a two-masted, double-ended Venetian fishing boat with gaily painted sails. Since the hull has very little draft forward, the sails are rigged so that the center of effort is further aft than usual.

BALANCE LUGSAIL

BOW LINES TO KEEP SAIL TAUT

BRIG :

Although a BARQUENTINE may be thought of as a diminutive BARQUE, and is indeed a development of that vessel, it is the other way round with Brig and BRIGANTINE. A BRIGANTINE is not a smaller Brig, rather, Brig is an abbreviation of BRIGANTINE which did eventually, however, become a type in its own right.

The progenitor, then, was the BRIGANTINE, which was often referred to as a Brig. But when the BRIGANTINE was combined with the SNOW, the new type thus formed was referred to as Brig, and henceforth this was the only meaning of Brig, except for the BRIG-SLOOP, which was in fact a BRIGANTINE.

BRIG : TWO-MASTED, SQUARE-RIGGED PLUS SPANKER AND CROSS-JACK
(BRIGANTINE CARRIES NO CROSS-JACK)

~ COLLIER BRIG

A British Collier Brig carried one huge headsail and very large top-sails. It was used in the 18th and 19th century coal trade on the east coast of England.

~ HERMAPHRODITE BRIG

Despite the name Brig this type might be arguably included under BRIGANTINE since it differs only in lacking the square topsails on the mainmast. On the other hand it is sometimes referred to as a Brig Schooner since it has obvious similarities to a SCHOONER, lacking only a fore-and-aft sail on the foremast. In any event, a Hermaphrodite Brig is a two-masted vessel, square-rigged on the foremast and fore-and-aft rigged on the mainmast.

~ MAN-OF-WAR-BRIG

GUN PORTS

BRIGANTINE :
A Brigantine was the name given to vessels used by brigands, originally rowed and used in the Mediterranean. As brigandage spread to the north around the end of the 17th century the type of vessel used changed but the name remained the same and gradually came to refer exclusively to a two-masted sailing ship of the type shown below.

SPANKER
(FORE-AND-AFT SAIL)

BRIGANTINE 1770 (NOTE: NO 'COURSE' (SQUARE SAIL ON LOWER MAIN MAST)
AS WITH BRIG, SEE PREVIOUS ILLUSTRATIONS)

~ BRIG-SLOOP
The term Brig-Sloop was a rating (the next class below FRIGATE) in the Royal Navy during the 18th century. The vessel thus rated might well have been rigged as a BRIG, a Brigantine, or even a SLOOP. However, in time, Brig-Sloop came to mean any BRIG or Brigantine in the Royal Navy.

BRIXHAM TRAWLER .   see TRAWLER

BUCENTAUR   Bucentaur comes from the Italian,
                        'buzino d'oro', golden bark. It was
the traditional name of the state GALLEY of the doges of Venice.
These Bucentaurs were used in the annual procession commemor-
ating the victory of Doge Pietro Orseolo II over the Dalmatian
pirates in **1000**.   The last one was destroyed by the French in
1798 for its gold.

BUGALET   A Bugalet was a small, square-rigged
                       vessel used off the coast of Brittany in
the **17**th century.

BUGEYE The Bugeye, which gets its name from the old practice of painting an eye on both sides of the bow, was a larger development of the SKIPJACK, used for offshore fishing in the Chesapeake Bay area. Originally a workboat it was later distinctively rigged as a shallow-draught yacht with two leg-of-mutton sails. The masts also have a distinctive excessive rake aft.

BUMBOAT Originally a boat used to remove filth from boats in the Thames, Bumboat gets its name from the old Suffolk word, 'bumbay,' quagmire. In 1685 Trinity House issued regulations regarding these boats, which were also used to carry provisions. The word later meant exclusively a boat used to carry fruit and vegetables to boats lying in harbor.

FOUL ANCHOR

BUSS   The term Buss, in the **17**th and **18**th centuries, was synonomous with Dutch and English fishing boats in the North Sea. Basically a beamy, square-rigged vessel, it was used in the herring industry until supplanted by the handier KETCH.

BUTTERMAN SCHOONER . see SCHOONER

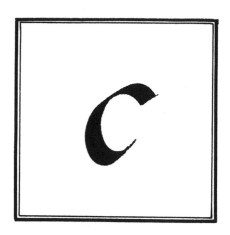

CABIN CRUISER .   see MOTORBOAT

CABLESHIP   A Cableship is a vessel fitted for laying
                    (and repairing)   underwater cables such as
telephone cable . One of the earliest Cableships was the **Great**
Eastern , launched in **1858** as a PASSENGER LINER , but subsequently
converted owing to her unsuitability as a trans-Atlantic passenger
ship.

CAIQUE   The word Caique comes from the Turkish word 'kaik,' meaning boat or skiff. Its original application was to the light rowboats used on the Bosphorus. It was also the name of the Sultan's ceremonial **BARGE**. It was then expanded to mean any light boat in the Levant.

      Caique now also refers to a small Levantine sailing vessel, although this use of the word has also been expanded to include small inter-island trading motor-vessels as far west as Greece and Corfu.

CÀIQUE   CURVED STEM

CALIFORNIA CLIPPER.   see CLIPPER

CAMSHIP   The name Cam comes from the initial letters of Catapult Aircraft Merchant ship. A Camship was a merchant ship in the Second World War, fitted with a catapult which could launch a fighter aircraft in the event the convoy, of which the Camship formed a part, was attacked by air.

      Unfortunately, the plane could not land on the Camship again and had to be ditched, hopefully nearby so that the pilot could be picked up.

CANOA

A Canoa is a **SLOOP**-rigged fishing boat of the ports around the Amazon delta in Brazil. Some are quite small (a few tons) and others are large enough to transport cattle from farms to Guyanne.

SHARPLY RAKED MAST AND STEM

CANOE:

A Canoe is a small open boat, originally by definition used by primitive peoples. The meaning was then extended to cover a large number of similar craft propelled by paddles. Some of these, for example many of the Pacific island craft listed below, are very large, taking up to thirty paddlers a side. As well as the primitive DUGOUT and skin canoes, there is now a large group of modern pleasure craft, many of which are designed for racing.

|← 14' (4.2 m.) →|

MODERN ALUMINUM CANOE (SIMILAR TO INDIAN BARK CANOE)

There are innumerable types of canoe, many of the more remarkable are listed here, some individually, and some under larger groupings such as Indian Canoes. Those listed individually are cross-referenced throughout the book, those included in large groups are not. A few other specialized canoes such as KAYAKS and UMIAKS are listed alphabetically throughout the book.

~ BANCA

A Banca is a double-outrigger Canoe from Mindanao Island in the Southern Philippines. Bamboo booms connect to long floats on both sides - these are the outriggers. The obliquely hung sail is set to a double mast, and is gaily painted and betasseled.

OUTRIGGERS

~ INDIAN CANOES

There was a great variety of skin and bark Canoes used by the different North American Indian tribes, admirably suited for the lake and river uses for which they were designed.

The Maine and Adirondack Canoes are the white man's development of the Indian's bark canoes.

ALGONQUIN BARK CANOE

CANADIAN BIRCHBARK CANOE

CHIPPEWA DUGOUT

HAIDA DUGOUTS

KOOTENAY SPRUCE BARK CANOE

AMERICAN
INDIAN
CANOES

~ LACCADIVE ISLANDS CANOE

The natives of the Laccadive Islands, which lie in the Indian Ocean to the west of India, use a DUGOUT canoe rigged with a large settee sail.

SETTEE SAIL

FORWARD RAKING MAST

~ LAPIL or LEPALEPA

The Lapil is a large (50' (15.2m)) DUGOUT sailing canoe from the area around North-west New Guinea. Lepalepa is an island variant of the same word, which actually simply means canoe.

~ LISI

A Lisi is a simple plank-built Canoe from the southeastern Solomon Islands. The washboards turn into high, carved and decorated peaks at each end.

WASHBOARD

~ MALAY OUTRIGGER CANOE

The Malay Outrigger, which is used in the Straits of Malacca, has remained unchanged for many centuries. It is double-ended, about **25'** (**7.6m**) long, and very narrow – only **9"** (**228mm**) wide. A pointed float is supported by two curved outrigger booms on the windward side, and under favorable conditions the boat is said to be able to make **20** knots.

~ MAORI WAR CANOE (WAKA TAUA)

The Maori War Canoe was a very large DUGOUT with the freeboard increased by washstrakes sewn to the hull. Both stem and sternpost were richly carved. Although the canoe was usually paddled, a V-shaped sail made of matting was sometimes used.

MATTING SAIL

STERN POST

WASHSTRAKE

STEM

70' (21.3m)

~ MON

Similar to the LISI and the ORA, the Mon is a plank-built canoe, with no outrigger. It comes from the Solomon Islands and was also used as a war canoe, being then much carved and decorated.

~ MTEPI

The Mtepi comes from the Lamu Islands, off the coast of Kenya, East Africa. It is a DUGOUT-type with a sail of matting set on upper and lower yards. The bowsprit carries a fringe of grass or reeds.

UPPER YARD

LOWER YARD

BOWSPRIT

~ ORA

The Ora is peculiar to San Cristobal Island in the Solomon Islands. Plank-built, with high peaks, it is similar to the MON.

NEW GUINEA

SOLOMON ISLANDS

PACIFIC

AUSTRALIA

NEW ZEALAND

~ OROU

The Orou is a trading and cargo vessel from Papua, New Guinea. It consists of two DUGOUT canoes joined by a deck of a width equal to half the length of the canoe. A mast is stepped in the larger of the two canoes and supports a 'crab-claw' oceanic lateen sail. When the Orou comes about, the steering paddle is unshipped and fixed on the opposite end of the boat, the vessel being thus reversible, bow becoming stern and stern becoming bow as the need arises.

~ SAMOAN CANOES

Like most other Pacific Island groups, Samoa has a variety of native canoes ranging from simple DUGOUTS to plank-built double canoes and canoes with outriggers. Among the different types, many of which are now not only obsolete but actually extinct, were the Paopao, a small outrigger for lagoon use; the Va'a'alo, a small outrigger used for fishing; the bigger Taumualua and the Fautasi, both without outriggers, paddled and sailed; and two large seagoing double canoes, the Va'a tele and the Alia. The Soatau, shown opposite, is a coasting craft, paddled and occasionally sailed.

SAMOAN SOATAU

~ TAHITIAN CANOES

There was an abundant variety of Tahitian Canoes, which included fishing craft, small lagoon Canoes and fifty-man war Canoes. The Canoe shown below, the Va'a motu, was a large outrigger capable of making long voyages. The Tipairua carried a thatched cabin. The Va'a ti'i was a large sacred Canoe, carved, decorated with feathers, and bearing shrines

TAHITIAN VA'A MOTU

~ TEPUKEI

The Tepukei, from the Matema Islands, east of the Solomon Islands, is a large sailing outrigger with the typical Oceanic 'crab-claw' sail. The actual canoe is very narrow, connected by a complicated arrangement of booms to the outrigger. On the larger models two floats were used. The platform slopes upwards and sometimes supports a thatched cabin.

CRAB-CLAW SAIL

PLATFORM

OUTRIGGER

~ THAMAKAU

One of the biggest (100' (30.4 m)) and best sailing outriggers, the Fijian Thamakau is, like other outriggers, reversible, since the actual outrigger must always be kept to windward to prevent overturning.

~ TONY   The Tony is an open sailing Canoe used for fishing out of Bombay, India. The hull is a DUGOUT, made from Malabar teak. The average length is about 31' (9.5 m).

SETTEE SAIL

~ TUINGUTU   The Tuingutu is an outrigger DUGOUT Canoe from the Tongan Archipelago in the Pacific. The rounded hull has washboards sewn to both sides.

~ UCHE

The word *Uche* simply means DUGOUT Canoe in the language of Hermit Islands, a small group west of the Admiralty Islands. However, the *Uche* is no small boat, being in fact a two-master, capable of carrying about fifty passengers.

~ VAKA

Vaka refers both to a simple one- or two-man outrigger Canoe from the Marquesas Islands and to a larger outrigger sailing DUGOUT Canoe from the Melanesian island of Rennel Island. The latter is distinguished by its long narrow sail which is hung from an inverted U-shaped mast.

VAKA

SAIL

MAST

OUTRIGGER

~ VANAGI   Although the vanagi is usually
paddled, and used as a fishing
boat, it can be fitted with one or two distinctive sails. It
comes from Port Moresby in Papua New Guinea.

~ WA   The Wa is related to the UCHE, and
comes from the Ninigo Islands, which lie
in the same direction as the Hermit Islands, home of the UCHE.
The Wa's sail is made from pandanus leaf, and the hull is
decorated with native designs.

~ WA'A

The Wa'a, a Hawaiian outrigger DUGOUT canoe, once existed in the thousands, but is now rare. In Captain Cook's time they were often fitted with Oceanic 'crab-claw' sails. Unlike many other outrigger canoes, whose outriggers are always to windward, whether the wind be over the port or starboard side, the Wa'a's outrigger is always on the port side.

~ WAGA

The Waga is another outrigger from Papua, common to the area between Mullens Harbor and Snau Island. The outrigger is as long as the canoe and is connected to it by ten booms, over which a platform is laid. The sail is made of plaited cocoanut leaves.

COCOANUT LEAF SAIL

BOOMS

CONNECTIVES

OUTRIGGER

~WAKA

North of the Solomon Islands (see map below illustration of ORA CANOE) lie the Taku Atoll Group — whence comes the Waka, a large heavy DUGOUT with sewn washstrakes and an oceanic Lateen sail.

CAPITAL SHIP

Capital ship is the term used in navies to denote the most important type of WARSHIP. During the age of sail the SHIP-OF-THE-LINE was the capital ship. When ships began to be built of iron and steel it was the BATTLESHIP and the DREADNOUGHT which was the capital ship. With the development of air power, the AIRCRAFT CARRIER became the capital ship but now even the CARRIER is virtually obsolescent and the nuclear missile-firing SUBMARINE is considered by many to be today's Capital ship.

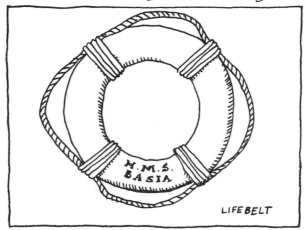

LIFEBELT

CARACORE

The Caracore is a large fast vessel used in the waters around Java, Celebes, Borneo, and New Guinea. Although it is a native craft, the Dutch used it as a coastal patrol craft because of its speed.

CARAVEL

The simplest definition of a Caravel is that of a relatively small trading vessel from the Mediterranean of the 14th to 17th centuries, which was also much used by the Spanish and Portuguese for exploration.

Beyond this the situation becomes confusing. For a start, the origin of the word is uncertain, although the origin of the type of vessel seems to have been a Portuguese form of lateen-rigged vessel similar to a boat still used on the Tagus, outside Lisbon, to this day.

By the second half of the 15th century there were Caravels in the North. That these vessels were carvel-built,

CARVEL PLANKING   FRAME OF HULL   CLINKER PLANKING

that is the planking was flush instead of the older overlapping style, known as clinker-built, has led some people to say that CARVEL is the same as Caravel, but no one really knows.

In any event, the Caravel was a vessel smaller than a SHIP and lacking the high forecastles and sterncastles of the larger contemporary CARRACKS. Although initially they were lateen-rigged (Caravela Latina), as was Columbus' **Niña** at the start of his American voyage in **1492**, many were rigged Caravela Rotunda, with square sails, and later on it was common for Caravels to be rigged in various combinations with three or four masts.

CARAVELA LATINA
(LATEEN-RIGGED)

CARAVELA ROTUNDA
(SQUARE-RIGGED)

CARAVEL 15th-16th CENT.

CAR FERRY . see   FERRY BOAT

CARGO LINER .   see CARGO SHIP

CARGO SHIP (FREIGHTER) :   A Cargo Ship is a vessel that carries cargo, or freight, rather than passengers, (and is neither a naval nor fishing vessel). This article classifies these vessels mainly by use, since the other system of classification, namely by construction, is one which overlaps not only within itself but with the employment to which the types may be put.

Before proceeding with the various types by use , here is a brief summary of the various types by construction and development.

Starting with **19**th century sailing ships, we find the most common type to have been the Flush-decked type, where the deck runs unbroken from stem to stern , with bridge and wheelhouse amidships.

FLUSH - DECK CARGO SHIP

By the end of the **19**th century it had been found that it was more practical to build a small anchor deck in the bow , and make the light bridge into a more substantial deckhouse. Such a vessel was the SCHOONER-rigged STEAMSHIP *Iberia*, built in 1881.

SCHOONER-RIGGED STEAMER *Iberia*

Since ships that carried a homogenous cargo rode too deeply in the bow, raised quarter-decks were built so that more cargo could be placed in the stern. Vessels on which the half deck had been extended forward were called Well-decked.

RAISED QUARTER-DECK VESSEL

WELL-DECKED VESSEL

The well-decked vessel could prove dangerous to the stability of the ship if swamped in heavy weather, however, and so the half-deck and the forecastle deck were joined, forming a hurricane deck, and thus completing the cycle back to a flush-decked vessel, but with much more freeboard.

HURRICANE-DECKED VESSEL

On some vessels the poop, or quarter deck, was joined to the bridge; these vessels being called 'Long Poopers', similar to well-decked vessels.

Shelter-deck vessels have a light, protective deck above the main deck, but the hatches of the shelter deck may not be battened down and the space between the two decks is considered to be part of the superstructure. If the hatches are battened down, then the vessel is called a closed shelter-deck vessel and the space between the two decks is included in the total tonnage.

WELL-DECKED VESSEL

LONG POOP VESSEL

- - - - DECK WITH UNBATTENED HATCHES
_____ MAIN CLOSED DECK

SHELTER DECK VESSEL

_____ CLOSED SHELTER
         DECK

- - - - - MAIN DECK
           (ALSO CLOSED)

CLOSED SHELTER
DECK VESSEL

Typical of many small TANKERS and coastal vessels are those with no bridge, all the machinery being aft-controlled from a long poop.

BRIDGE

POOP

FORECASTLE DECK

COASTAL VESSEL

A Cargo Ship with poop, bridge, and forecastle may be called a Three Island vessel since when the hull is down behind the horizon, or a heavy swell, it is only the three superstructures that may be seen.

THREE ISLAND VESSEL

~ CARGO LINER   A Freighter which plies a regular route, like a PASSENGER LINER, is said to be a Cargo Liner — and since her route is regular, passengers may be carried.   Consequently, Cargo Liners usually have accommodation for a number of passengers. Such a vessel is the French ship, **Magellan**, which carries a crew of fifty-seven and twelve passengers in the Pacific.

Magellan   490' (150 m.)

~ COLLIER

The first vessels to carry cargoes of coal were the 17th and 18th century COLLIER BRIGS. These sturdy sailing ships (so strong, in fact, that they were the vessels that Captain Cook, who had been first apprenticed to the sea in them, selected as his ships for his voyages of exploration in 1768-1780) could carry from 300 to 400 tons of coal.

Modern Colliers can carry as much as 25,000 tons. The illustration below, however, is of a much smaller ship used to carry the same North Country coal to London as did the original COLLIER BRIGS.

~ CONTAINER SHIP

A container Ship is a Cargo Ship built expressly for the carriage of cargo pre-packed in standardized containers; each container holding 18 tons of cargo. Thus holds and deck space are designed exactly to accommodate the containers. This is supposed to eradicate the danger of cargo shifting at sea, and control the balance of the ship. However, the practice of carrying additional containers on deck often nullifies this advantage.

~ LIBERTY SHIP

Built to a design originally produced in England by the Sunderland Company, in **1879**, Liberty ships were built in U.S. shipyards to replace tonnage sunk by German, Italian, and Japanese U-Boats during the second World War. A total of **2,770** of these merchant ships were built, including some equipped as COLLIERS and TANKERS. Their main features were extreme simplicity of design and rapidity of construction.

LIBERTY SHIP

LENGTH : 441·5' (134·5 m)   WIDTH : 57' (17·4 m)

2,500 H.P. STEAM ENGINES — SPEED : 11 KNOTS

~ REFRIGERATOR SHIP

Refrigerator ships are used for the transport of meat, fruit, fish, and dairy products, and their holds are equipped wholly or partly as refrigerators. They are generally fairly fast vessels, often capable of making as much as **16** knots. Since insulating material is expensive the holds are not very deep and are rarely used for other cargoes.

TILLER OF GOKSTAD VIKING SHIP
A.D. 900

~ TRAMP

A Tramp is a cargo-carrying merchant vessel which, in distinction to a CARGO LINER, does not work a regular route but carries cargo to any port as desired. Although the modern Tramp does not sell her cargo but merely transports it for others, she is the descendant of the old merchant adventurer who would sell his goods at various ports and load other goods to carry home.

~ TURRET DECK VESSEL

Although Turret Deck Vessels are strictly a type by construction, and this section is primarily devoted to types of freighters by use, they are included here because the name is so important, and they are actually used solely for carrying bulk cargo.

Bulk cargo, such as ore and grain, poses special problems of dangerous shifting. In **1892** the ship **Turret** was built to combat these problems. The solution was to build a vessel with sides that swept in to form a side deck, and then continued up to a narrower deck where the hatches were. Similar vessels were thereafter called Turret Deck Vessels. Nowadays a related type – Trunk Deck Vessel – is used for ore.

s.s. Turret   1892

TURRET DECK VESSEL

SECTION AMIDSHIPS

TRUNK DECK VESSEL

~ VICTORY SHIP

When the LIBERTY SHIPS were built, turbine engines were reserved for naval use, but towards the end of the Second World War a less spartan design was adopted to replace merchant ships sunk by the enemy. This design was the Victory Ship, equipped with a turbine engine, a longer hull, and a forecastle.

VICTORY SHIP
LENGTH : 455' (138.5 m)   WIDTH : 61.5' (18.7 m)
8,500 H.P. TURBINE ENGINES   SPEED : 16½ KNOTS

CARRACK

The Carrack was a large trading vessel of both northern and southern Europe from the 14th to the 17th century. It was developed from the typically northern square rig and the typically southern lateen rig. Similar to the CARAVEL, the Carrack was beamier, larger, and built with high fore- and aft-castles. It was in fact, the forerunner of the three-masted SHIP – the major influence in naval architecture until the advent of the steam engine in the 19th century.

Early Carracks had a mainmast and a small mizzen, used for steering purposes only, but gradually three-masters became the rule, square-rigged on the fore and main, and lateen-rigged on the mizzen.

They were also the first ships to regularly carry guns, making them heavily armed merchant vessels. see also ARGOSY.

15TH CENTURY CARRACK

CARTEL   A Cartel was the ship used in time of war to negotiate between enemies. To signify that a ship was a Cartel, a white flag would be flown which guaranteed immunity for the ship. Ships' boats, also flying the white flag, were sometimes used as Cartels too.

CARVEL   Used in the late Middle Ages, the Carvel was a small, two-masted, lateen-rigged vessel, used for small cargoes in the Mediterranean. It is considered a separate craft, though some think it is a synonym for the CARAVEL.

CASCO   Casco is the local name for a square-ended, flat-bottomed boat used in the Philippine Islands as a LIGHTER for transporting cargo between ship and shore.

CAT   Cat is a word which has been much used in the nautical vocabulary; with regard to vessels the various meanings are:

a.   A Cat was a rowing vessel, with **50** oars or sweeps on either side, two men to an oar, the vessel having a beak like a GALLEY.

6.   In the early **18**th century, Cat referred to a blunt-bowed (and therefore rather slow) three-masted merchant vessel similar to a Dutch FLUTE.

c.   Cat sometimes means the small, open sailing boat known in America as a CAT BOAT and in Britain as an UNA BOAT (see CAT BOAT).

d.   The sailing collier used in northern Europe until the mid-**19**th century, and which was modeled after a

Norwegian vessel with a canoe stern, projecting quarters and a deep waist, was known as a cat. Most noticeable was the absence of a figurehead, in the days when even the smallest boat bore some decoration.

17TH - 18TH CENT. NORWEGIAN CAT

CATAMARAN

Catamaran comes from two Tamil words, 'katta', to tie, and 'maram', wood.

a.   The original meaning thus was of a raft of three or five logs lashed together used by the natives of Ceylon. It also referred to a larger but similar craft used as a surf boat in both the East and West Indies.

b.   The second meaning of Catamaran refers to a short-lived British invention launched in **1804**. This was a long, lead-lined box loaded with explosives, which was intended to hook onto moored vessels' lines and, with the aid of a clockwork timing mechanism, explode five minutes later. The French, for whom they had been designed, quickly rendered them ineffective by the use of booms and chain cables.

c.   The third meaning of Catamaran is of a small rectangular craft designed to lie alongside larger vessels and protect them from the jetties to which they are moored.

d.   Catamaran finally, and now most commonly, means a twin-hulled racing or cruising pleasure craft, which, by virtue of its low immersion area, is considerably faster than traditional mono-hulls. See also MULTI-HULL.

TWIN HULLS

— 16' (5.05m) —

CAT BOAT (UNA BOAT)

The Cat Boat originated in America around the Cape Cod region, for fishing in shallow waters, in the mid-19th century. These boats are very beamy and shallow, with big rudders and a mast stepped in the bows.

In 1852, a Cat Boat called **Una** was shipped to Cowes in England and gave her name to the type in England. Some of the later, racing models set a foresail on a long bowsprit.

CENTERBOARD

CAT SCHOONER.   see SCHOONER

CENTERBOARD SCHOONER.   see SCHOONER

CHANNEL ISLANDER

The Channel Islander was a fishing boat and PILOT BOAT common around the Channel Islands in the English Channel. Around **36'** (**11m**) long and three-masted, the rig changed from the original lugsail to a boomless fore-and-aft gaff sail.

BOOMLESS
FORE-AND-AFT SAILS

CHASSE-MARÉE

Chasse-marée means sea hunter and refers to a fast French LUGGER used both by French customs and smugglers. During the Napoleonic Wars the Chasse-marée was used as a dispatch boat. Later, many were commissioned as PRIVATEERS. However, she suffered from the fact that a large crew was needed to handle the considerable sail area and to man the guns, plus the fact that when running before the wind she could be easily overtaken by a ship with the normal square rig.

Unlike the chasse-marée illustrated on the next page, some of the larger vessels could even carry a lug topsail set on the mainmast.

FRENCH CHASSE-MARÉE

CHEBACCO BOAT

The Chebacco Boat originated in the Parish of Chebacco of Ipswich, now part of Essex, Massachusetts, after the Revolutionary War. It was the forerunner of the PINKY, and caught most of New England's fish. It was characterized by the overhanging 'pink' stern and CAT SCHOONER rig — no bowsprit or headsails.

PINK STERN

CHEBECK .   see SHEBEK

CHESAPEAKE BAY SCHOONER .   see SCHOONER

CHINESE DUGOUT .   see DUGOUT

CHINESE JUNK .   see JUNK

CIRCULAR VESSEL .   see POPOFFKA

CLIPPER (CLIPPER SHIP):   Clipper is a word used very loosely to describe types of very fast sailing ships. In fact, the term is said to have originated because of the ability of certain fast ships to clip, or shorten, the regular passage time.

The first ships to be described as clippers - the BALTIMORE CLIPPERS - were actually SCHOONERS. Various aspects of these ships were gradually combined with those of larger, square-riggers until, in 1845, the first true clipper ship was built in New York. This was the **Rainbow**.

The fully developed clipper may be characterized by a raking stem and an overhanging stern - thus reducing the area of hull in contact with the water - and a lofty, heavily sparred rig carrying a larger area of sail than other ships.

The discovery of gold in California in 1848, in Australia in 1850, and the opening of the China-to-London tea trade in 1849 boosted American production of clippers until the depression of 1857 and the American Civil War (1861-1865) resulted in the supremacy of British shipyards.

Flying Cloud : 1851
FASTEST AMERICAN CLIPPER , NEW YORK – SAN FRANCISCO, 89 DAYS
209.5' (63.8 m) L.W.L.

~ BALTIMORE CLIPPER

The Baltimore Clipper was
a speedy SCHOONER which

originated in Baltimore and became famous as a blockade runner and a PRIVATEER in the war of 1812, and later as a SLAVER. It was marked by the extreme rake of the masts and a hull deeper aft than foreward.

~ CALIFORNIA CLIPPER

California Clippers were those Clippers which traveled from New York to San Francisco round Cape Horn during the decade following the California gold rush in 1848. On the return trip they often brought tea and spices from China. The **Flying Cloud**, shown on the previous page, was one of the most famous California Clippers.

~ HALF CLIPPER

Half Clippers were designed to carry more cargo than full Clipper Ships, and were consequently not as fast. They were popular in the 1870's and 1880's when operation of the extreme Clippers began to be uneconomical owing to their lower freight rates.

~ OPIUM CLIPPER

Like the BALTIMORE CLIPPER, the Opium Clipper wasn't actually a clipper at all; for the most part Opium Clippers were BRIGS, SCHOONERS, and BARQUES.

They were small, extremely fast ships, used to carry illicit opium from India to China from about 1830 to 1855.

Since they had to contend with typhoons, pirates, armed JUNKS, and hostile Mandarins, they carried only small amounts of cargo - to minimize any loss - and were equipped with oars and cannon.

~ TEA CLIPPER   In 1849 the British Navigation Acts were repealed, opening the tea trade, from China to London, to foreign ships. The first American vessel to unload tea in England was the **Oriental**, which was so much faster a ship that she was at once chartered at $30 a ton, while the slower British ships received less than $20 a ton. This immediately stimulated British construction of Clipper ships, culminating in the great **Cutty Sark** and the **Thermopylae**, probably the two most outstanding Tea Clippers ever built.

For more than twenty years, annual tea races were held – the most famous being in 1866 when the **Fiery Cross** left Foochow on May 29th, the **Ariel**, **Taeping**, and **Serica** on the 30th, and the **Taitsing** on the 31st; the **Taeping**, **Ariel**, and **Serica** all arrived in London on September 6th, the **Fiery Cross** and **Taitsing** two days later.

The opening of the Suez Canal and the need for ships with smaller crews eventually contributed to the demise of these fastest sailing ships of all time.

BOW AND FIGUREHEAD OF THE *Cutty Sark*

~ WOOL CLIPPER

With the opening of the Suez Canal and the coincident rapid development of trade between Britain and her colonies in the 1870's the TEA CLIPPERS turned to the Australian wool trade.

However, still more ships were needed and more ships were built — bigger, and with steel hulls, spars, and rigging. Since it was now soon found that ships over 1,500 tons were uneconomical to run owing to the large crews needed, a new type of vessel evolved, rigged usually as BARQUE or SHIP.

Thus the Wool clippers were not strict clippers, but represented the final development of the 'Age of Sail' before steam took over.

Preussen
FIVE-MASTED FULL-RIGGED SHIP
407.8' (124.2 m) LONG

CLIPPER FISHERMAN. SEE SCHOONER, GLOUCESTER FISHING

COASTAL MOTOR BOAT or **C.M.B.** The Coastal Motor Boat was a type of small WARSHIP used during the First World War. There were two sizes,

30′ (12 m) and 55′ (16.7 m), with speeds of 30 knots and 42 knots respectively. They carried mines, torpedoes, and anti-submarine depth charges.

COASTER   The word Coaster may be applied to any vessel employed in a coastwise trade. such as COBLES, KETCHES, LUGGERS, or CRABBERS.

HIGHLAND COASTER SLOOP

LUGGER
(CORNISH)

101

COBLE   The Coble is a flat-bottomed, carvel-built
                fishing boat common to the north-east coast
of England. It features a deep forefoot enabling it to be
launched bow-first into the sea. Sailed with a single
dipping lugsail and sometimes a jib on a temporary bowsprit, it
is fitted for rowing with three pairs of oars.

It was in a Coble that Grace Darling and her father, the
lighthouse-keeper, made the daring and celebrated rescue of the
crew of the **Forfarshire** when she wrecked off the Outer
Farne Island light in **1838**.

DEEP RUDDER   DEEP FOREFOOT

COCK BOAT   Originally, all boats carried on board a
                     ship were known as Cockboats, or Cocks.
This is thus the origin of the naval term coxswain (originally
cockswain), for the coxswain was the helmsman and man
in charge of the ship's boat.

A cockboat is thus a small DINGHY or rowboat used
as a TENDER.

COD-BANGER Boats which used lines as opposed to trawls when fishing for cod were known as Cod-bangers in the **19**th century.

COG The Cog was the merchant ship of the **13**th to **15**th centuries. A northern, clinker-built vessel with a square sail, rounded bow and stern and broad beam, it was the ship most used by the Hansa League.

BASIC COG HULL

BALTIC COG 1350

COLLIER .   see CARGO SHIP

COLLIER BRIG .   see BRIG

COLONIAL FISHING VESSEL   Although this is a very general term, Colonial Fishing vessel nevertheless can be used to describe the kind of vessel used in the American east coast fisheries in the 17th century.   They were generally carvel-built, with a single square sail and a jib, averaging about 40' (12m) long.

CONTAINER SHIP .   see CARGO SHIP .

CONTINENTAL GALLEY .   see GALLEY

CORACLE

A coracle was originally a small boat made of skins over a wicker frame, in use by the ancient Britons even before the advent of the Romans. Similar to the Irish CURRAGH, the Coracle is still found in Wales, where it is now made from canvas and used as a one-man river fishing boat.

STRAP FOR CARRYING
CORACLE ON BACK

CORBITA

The Corbita was the merchant ship of Imperial Rome. Large and heavily built, the Corbita could carry up to **400** tons of cargo. In addition to the single square sail, she also set two raffee topsails and a small square sail on an artemon mast over the bows.

RAFFEE TOPSAIL

ARTEMON MAST

CORSAIR

Corsairs, regarded by many people as pirates, were usually legitimate **PRIVATEERS**, licensed by the Turkish government at Constantinople, to prey on the merchant shipping of various Christian states. They cruised off the Mediterranean coast of North Africa until as late as **1825**. They were thus private ships of various designs.

CORVETTE

The Corvette was a flush-decked **WARSHIP** of the **17**th and **18**th centuries, one class below **FRIGATES**. Ship-rigged on three masts and with a single tier of guns, the hull form was a development of the **GALLEY**. The English Corvettes were often called **SLOOP-OF-WARS** and were often rigged as either **BRIGS** or **SCHOONERS**.

SHIP-SLOOP OR
CORVETTE

During the Second World War, Corvette was used again as a class name for an anti-submarine **ESCORT VESSEL**

CRABBER Crabbers are small, open boats used for setting out and collecting crab pots. The rig and size of these boats varies from locality to locality.

CRAFT Craft is a word which has many meanings, but its nautical one derives from the fact that in the 15th, 16th, and 17th centuries, any kind of line, net, or hook used for catching fish was called a craft. In consequence, small fishing vessels such as **HOYS**, **KETCHES**, and **BUSSES** became known as small craft. Nowadays the term has been expanded to include all small vessels, whether they are fishing craft or not.

CROMSTER A Cromster was a two-masted Elizabethan vessel used in England and Holland, where it was known as a Cromsteven.

16TH CENTURY CROMSTER

CRUISER

a.   Cruiser, originally spelled Cruizer, was at first any ship, often a **FRIGATE**, detached from a fleet for independent reconnaissance. The important similarity of such ships was that they be fast and superior sailers.

b.   With steam propulsion and armour plating in the **19**th century, Cruisers became a generic type of **WARSHIP** in their own right. Filling roughly the place of the **FRIGATE** in the sailing navies, strong but swift, cruisers were built in several categories. Biggest were Armoured Cruisers (**16,000** tons); then came Belted Cruisers (with armour only at the waterline); Second Class Cruisers (with only light armour); and Light Cruisers, with virtually no armour but very fast.

     By the First World War there were many specialized types of Cruisers, including the Large Armoured Cruiser, which was actually a **BATTLESHIP**, and which accordingly had its name changed to **BATTLE-CRUISER**.

     Since aerial reconnaissance has taken over most of the Cruiser's original duties, the modern Cruiser is now often an independent miniature **BATTLESHIP** or **AIRCRAFT CARRIER**, equipped with missiles instead of guns.

Königsberg : 1907
383' (116.7m) LONG : SPEED 25.7 KNOTS

C.   The term Cruiser is now also applied to a great many sailing and power YACHTS used for long- or short-distance cruising. Provided such boats have overnight accommodations, they are all known as Cruisers.

CRUISING YACHT.   see YACHT

CUNNER   A Cunner, also known by the more descriptive name Chesapeake Bay Dugout Canoe, is a CAT-SCHOONER-rigged boat, about **25'** (**7.6m**) long, used in the Chesapeake Bay oyster fisheries.

CURRACH or **CURRAGH**   The Currach is a very old boat peculiar to Ireland, very similar to the **CORACLE**, being originally made of skins, but now constructed with canvas over a light frame. Currachs are more boat-shaped than **CORACLES**, but equally light. Usually small, they are sometimes made with eight oars and a small square sail.

They are particularly associated with the Aran Islands of the west coast of Ireland, carrying not only people, but goods and cattle.

CUTTER :

a.   The older meaning of Cutter was the fast rig shown below, introduced about **1740**, used mainly as auxiliaries to the war fleets and as REVENUE CUTTERS.

GAFF MAINSAIL

SQUARE TOPSAIL

TWO JIBS

b.   The second meaning of Cutter is a clinker-built ship's boat up to **30'(9m)** long, with eight to fourteen oars, originally rigged with two masts carrying a dipping lug foresail, and a standing lug mainsail. What the connection is between the larger cutter and the ship's cutter is unclear.

c.   In the modern pleasure-sailing world a Cutter means a sailing YACHT with a mainsail and two foresails – except in the U.S.A. where the term is reserved for the old-fashioned rig with topsail and a very long bowsprit. The two types are shown opposite.

TOPSAIL

GAFF MAINSAIL

MODERN CUTTER — AMERICAN
DEFINITION — OLD-STYLE RIG

TWO FORESAILS

LONG BOWSPRIT

BERMUDA RIG
MAINSAIL

TWO FORESAILS

MODERN CUTTER YACHT

111

a.　　A cutter can also be a steam vessel of about **2,000** tons in the U.S. Navy used by the U.S. Coast Guard or Weather Patrol; or a steam or diesel light TENDER used by Trinity House.

~ PILOT CUTTER　　Cutter-rigged vessels, being fast and handy, were much used as PILOT BOATS before the introduction of steam. Shown below is a Dutch Pilot Cutter from the **1880**'s.

~REVENUE CUTTER　　Owing to high import taxes, smuggling became very profitable during the late **18**th and early **19**th centuries. Consequently, fast, armed vessels were needed by various governments to catch the smugglers. In England the Topsail Cutter was employed, armed with ten nine-pound guns. In America, however, Revenue Cutters were actually SCHOONERS.

18 TH CENT.

CUTTER GALLEY

The Cutter Galley was a small GALLEY, about **43'** (**13m**) long, rigged as a CUTTER with square topsails. The Cutter Galley was one of the variously rigged GALLEYS used in the American revolutionary war.

AMERICAN CUTTER GALLEY 1776

Sloop.

Here is a fine view of a large sloop, in full sail, ploughing the waves as she goes. These vessels are well known to most young people who live in towns near the sea, or large rivers ; but to children particularly who dwell far in the country, this picture will be interesting. These sloops carry passengers and produce, and return from market with merchandise. The sail in front is called the jib, the large one is the mainsail, and that high up is the topsail; on the extreme height is fixed the streamer.

DAHABIA or **DAHABIAH** or **DAHABEEYAH**   This word comes from the Arabic word, 'dahabiyah,' meaning golden, for originally the Dahabia was a gilded STATE BARGE used by Egyptian rulers. Nowadays, motor vessels are used where previously the Dahabia was the luxury boat of the Nile with passenger accommodation and sun roof.

DAGO BOAT

Although later referred to as a FELUCCA, the Dago Boat, a small, lateen-rigged fishing boat, was so known by all who used her. Common on the California coast around the turn of the last century, the Dago Boat is thought to have originated around Naples.

DAMELOPRE

Damelopre was a word which pertained to those Dutch sailing BARGES or COASTERS in which the mast was stepped in a tabernacle so that it could be lowered when passing under bridges.

MAST

TABERNACLE

DANDY: Dandy was a term applied by British fisherman to any KETCH or YAWL; although properly a true Dandy is lug-rigged, fore-and-aft mainsails are also used.

DANDY

KETCH-RIGGED DANDY

~ BALTIC DANDY The true KETCH has a mizzen sail about half the size of the main sail; the true YAWL has a mizzen sail about one-quarter the size of the mainsail; the true Dandy has a mizzen sail (called the Dandy) about one-third the size of the mainsail. The Baltic Dandy has a much bigger mizzen mast and carries more sail, so that sometimes it looks almost like a SCHOONER, especially when square sails are also carried on the mainmast. Nevertheless, the Baltic Dandy is essentially KETCH-rigged.

A KETCH carries a mainsail, and a smaller mizzen sail forward of the steering gear.

MAINSAIL

MIZZEN SAIL

STEERING GEAR

BALTIC DANDY

DAYSAILER .   see YACHT

DEAL LUGGER .   see LUGGER

DESTROYER   Destroyers, which were first developed in the
                      1890's, were originally known as TORPEDO BOAT
Destroyers, since this was their function . They later grew in size,
speed, and duty, and are now used for a wide range of naval tasks.

GERMAN HEAVY DESTROYER Karl Gaster
LENGTH: 410' (125m)
SPEED: 38 KNOTS

118

DESTROYER ESCORT.   see FRIGATE

DE WANG

The De Wang is a two-masted sailing dugout CANOE from the Sassi Islands in the Bismarke Archipelago off New Guinea. The hull, which is usually surmounted by a platform, has sharp beaks at both ends. There is a heavy outrigger, and the sails, set on oppositely raking masts, are made from pandanus leaves.

BEAK   BEAK

DGHAISA

The Dghaisa (pronounced Dicer) is a Maltese passenger boat much like a GONDOLA, usually rowed by two standing oarsmen (who push rather than pull) but sometimes sailed with a single lateen sail. Dghaisas from Valetta, the capital of Malta, are highly decorated and gaily painted.

GONDOLA PROW

DHOW : Although there is no vessel actually called Dhow by the Arabs themselves, most of the large Arabian vessels are called Dhows by Europeans. They are characterized in general by lateen sails, sharp, overhanging bows, and high, square sterns. The Baghla, Boom, and Ghanja, which sail the waters around Arabia, are typical 'Dhows.'

BAGHLA

~ BATELO (BATEELE) The Batelo is a small Dhow, about **50' (15m)** long, with a beam about **10' (3m)** — most Dhows have broad beams.

120

~ GARUKHA

The Garukha is a Dhow-type craft from the Persian Gulf. Its chief peculiarity lies in its steering gear, which consists not of a tiller or wheel, but of two spars protruding from the quarters, and connected to the rudder by running tackle.

~ GEHAZI

The Gehazi is a high-pooped Dhow used on the African coast as far south as Zanzibar and is related to the SAMBUK.

~ KOTIA

The Kotia, related to the PATTAMAR, is an Indian Dhow from the Malabar coast. The square transom stern is often heavily carved and the stem invariably carries a parrot beak.

STEERED BY A WHEEL

JIB

PARROT BEAK

MALABAR KOTIA

~ PATTAMAR

The Pattamar is a large two- or three- masted Dhow from the Coromandel coast of Eastern India, usually red and black with a globe painted on the transom.

THREE-MASTED PATTAMAR

~ SAMBUK

The Sambuk, used in the Red Sea, bears such striking resemblance to old CARAVELS that some early European influence must be assumed.

~ ZARUG or ZARUK

The Zarug and its close relative, the Badan, are double-enders, and apart from the lateen sail have little in common with other Dhows, presumably having suffered less European influence. Common in the waters around Aden, they were much used by smugglers and slave-traders.

123

DINGI or **DINGHI**   Dingi, which comes from the Hindi, 'dengi' or 'dingi,' is the name of the small, open-hulled boat used on the Ganges and Hugli Rivers in India, and from which our word DINGHY comes.

Sailed with a simple square sail and steered with a sweep, the boat looks a lot like early Egyptian craft.

DINGHY: First used as general work boats or tenders to WARSHIPS and merchant vessels, Dinghies were fitted with sails, and after the First World War became enormously popular as small racing boats, there now being over **300** classes of racing Dinghies.

TYPICAL 12' (3.5m)
SAILING DINGHY

~ BAHAMA DINGHY   The typical small workboat of
the Bahamas was referred to as
a Bahama Dinghy. Varying in size from 13' (4m.) to 20' (7m)
long, these boats were variously rigged with different kinds of
mainsails, some carrying jibs as well.

BAHAMA MAINSAIL

HEART-SHAPED TRANSOM

TRANSOM

CAT-RIGGED BAHAMA DINGHY

DISPATCH BOAT   A small naval vessel used for
carrying messages or dispatches from
ship to ship.

DOGGER   The Dogger was a Dutch TRAWLER which fished
the North Sea in the Middle Ages and which
gave its name to the Dogger Bank, a large shallow area much
frequented by fisherman from all the surrounding countries.

In the mid-17th century a KETCH-type
fishing vessel which worked the Dogger Bank also became known
as a Dogger. This is the type illustrated on the next page.

18TH CENTURY DUTCH DOGGER

DONKEY FRIGATE. see FRIGATE

DORY   Although the name Dory has recently been given to a type of hard-chine DINGHY often fitted with an outboard and used as a workboat, it was originally a flat-bottomed boat with removable thwarts, enabling it to be stacked in piles on the Newfoundland fishing boats from which it was used to catch the fish.

REMOVABLE THWARTS

FISHING DORY

DOUARNENEZ LUGGER.   see LUGGER

DOUBLE CANOE   The Double Canoe, a craft once
                               common in the Pacific, is a
cross between CANOE, DUGOUT, and the modern CATAMARAN.
It was made by joining two CANOES, usually DUGOUTS, and not
always of the same length, together with short booms.
Usually equipped for sailing, they ranged from the simple
Wa'a kaulua of Hawaii to the large, ocean-going Tipairua
of the society Islands.

PAHI DOUBLE CANOE , TUAMOTU ARCHIPELAGO

DOUBLE TOPSAIL SCHOONER.   see SCHOONER

DRAGON.   see VIKING LONGSHIP

DRAKAR

The Drakar was the Danish version of the VIKING LONGSHIP. Called Drakar from the custom of carving a dragon at the stemhead (and often continuing the carving the length of the ship with the tail at the sternpost), Drakars first attacked England in **787** and continued for over a hundred years until Canute, King of Denmark, became King of England.

DREADNOUGHT

Dreadnought was the name given to fast, heavily armoured and armed BATTLESHIPS, based on the then revolutionary British **H.M.S. Dreadnought** built in **1906**.

GERMAN DREADNOUGHT

128

DREDGER
A Dredger is a vessel designed to deepen waterways. There are suction Dredgers, but the most common kind employ an endless chain of buckets which scoop up the bottom and discharge it onto waiting LIGHTERS. For shallow waters a HOVERCRAFT Dredger has been developed.

BUCKETS

DRIFTER :
A Drifter is a fishing boat, usually fitted with steam or diesel engines today, which catches fish with drift nets.

Drift nets, supported by cork or plastic floats, are hung across the expected path of fish which swim in shoals near the surface, such as herring.

DRIFT NET

~ BOULOGNE DRIFTER

The Boulogne Drifter was a KETCH-rigged vessel, working from the port of Boulogne in France, engaged in the drift net fishing industry. Up to **90'** (**27m**) long, these boats are a good example of the large sailing Drifters used before motor propulsion became the rule.

DROMON

The word Dromon is Greek and means runner, although some maintain that it is Byzantine in origin and denoted a royal ship. It seems to have been, along with the **SELANDER**, the ship that replaced the Roman **TRIREME**, and was used in the Mediterranean until the Middle Ages. The name is most often used to refer to any large ship of that period propelled by oars or sail and used as a transporter of goods or soldiers. The ships that carried the Christian armies to the Crusades were called Dromons, or Dromonds.

DUGOUT : The Dugout is a primitive form of CANOE which has been made and used since prehistoric times. A log is burnt or otherwise hollowed out, and paddled, either by hand or paddles.

Dugouts may be found all over the world from China to Scandinavia and from North America to the Pacific.

STONE AGE SCANDINAVIAN DUGOUT

~CHINESE DUGOUT As an example of how different Dugouts can be, the illustration below shows a Chinese Dugout from a drawing made at the beginning of the 19th century.

DUKW   DUKW was the code name for a military amphibious vehicle used in the second World War. Its full name was Amphibian Vehicle All-Wheel Drive Dual Rear Axle, and it could cross rivers and estuaries as well as drive on land.

DUM   The Dum was a fishing boat used from the Dutch harbor of Scheveningen. Very beamy and with a shallow draught, it had leeboards like many other Dutch craft.

DUMB VESSEL   A Dumb Vessel is simply any vessel with no means of self-propulsion, such as a LIGHTER.

DUTCH BARGE.   see BARGE

DYNASHIP   Dynaships are being designed to return to wind power, due to the increasing cost of oil. Square sails, aerodynamically designed, and operated by electro-hydraulic means from the bridge by one man, will be **60**% more efficient than in the days of the old square-riggers.

Dynaships will, of course, have an auxiliary engine in order to get to areas of maximum wind, as predicted by satellites. Bulk carriers of up to **17,000** tons are being planned.

A SHIP

19TH century British woodcut

EAST INDIAMAN   The ships that were built by the various East India trading companies, especially the British and the Dutch, were collectively known as East Indiamen. They were large, armed, and often sumptuous vessels. For more than two hundred years they were the ne plus ultra of shipping.

BRITISH EAST INDIAMAN 1730

E - BOAT.   see   TORPEDO BOAT, MOTOR

EGYPTIAN CRAFT   The earliest known picture of any Egyptian craft, which dates no less than **4,000** B.C., suggests something like the illustration below.

EGYPTIAN SHIP   4000 B.C.

Two and a half thousand years later, which still only brings us to **1500** B.C., we have more accurate and reliable pictures of Egyptian craft. These come from temple carvings celebrating Queen Hatshepsut's voyage to the Land of Punt, which may have been Somaliland.

ROPE TRUSS

SUPPORTED BY CRUTCHES

STEERING OARS

EGYPTIAN SHIP   1500 BC.

ENDROL

The Endrol is a DUGOUT sailing CANOE peculiar to the Admiralty Islands in the Bismark Archipelago of New Guinea. The ends of the hollowed-out hull are plugged with long blocks of wood carved in the shape of crocodiles. One- or two-masted, the bigger Endrols are manned by as many as fifteen men.

OUTRIGGER

ESSEX OYSTER BOAT

The Essex Oyster Boat was once common in ports around the Thames estuary. Similar to the BAWLEY, the mainsail is higher, giving this CUTTER-rigged boat a more YACHT-like appearance.

ESCORT VESSEL

An Escort Vessel may be any ship — such as a TRAWLER, SLOOP, CUTTER, or FRIGATE, etc. — whose duty in time of war is the protection of single ships or convoys from submarine, surface, or air attack.

ESNECCA (SNEKKJA)

The Scandinavian meaning of Snekkja is snake, and thus it is thought that an Esnecca was a longer form of VIKING LONGSHIP, although no pictorial evidence remains to support this idea.

During the 12th century various English kings had Esneccas, which were then the equivalent of a ROYAL YACHT.

ETAPLES LUGGER.   see LUGGER

EXPLOSION VESSEL

There have been many famous Explosion Vessels, which are simply usually old or obsolescent vessels used for destroying things, such as other ships or barricades, with which they come into contact, by exploding themselves.

One of the more recent examples was the old DESTROYER H.M.S. Campbletown, which rammed and exploded against the dock caissons at St. Nazaire in 1942.

FAST PATROL BOAT

The Fast Patrol Boat was a development, after the Second World War, of the MOTOR GUNBOAT, designed for naval warfare in coastal waters. Instead of gasoline engines, gas turbines are used, producing speeds of up to **40** knots, and instead of torpedos, small guided missiles are often used.

FELUCCA

The Felucca is a Mediterranean vessel which comes in many shapes and sizes. Some are quite small and rowed; others, usually lateen-rigged, may be two-masted and seagoing.

LARGE SPANISH FELUCCA : 1800

FERRY:

A Ferry is designed to transport people and goods from one place to another, usually a short distance, on a regular schedule. Ferries range from platforms hauled across rivers on cables to large vessels crossing the North Sea.

HUDSON RIVER FERRY

~ CAR FERRY

Most large passenger Ferries have facilities for automobiles, such as the Car Ferry **Compiègne**, which runs between Calais and Dover, and can carry **164** cars. However, many smaller passenger Ferries are now being replaced by HYDROFOILS.

CAR FERRY Compiègne : 1958   1,000 PASSENGERS
164 AUTOMOBILES

~ TRAIN FERRY

Some Ferries are specially designed so that train carriages may be ferried from coast to coast. One of the biggest of these is the train Ferry **Trelleborg** which carries **40** railroad cars from Trelleborg to Sasnitz.

TRAIN FERRY Trelleborg : 1958   40 RAILROAD CARS
30 AUTOMOBILES
1,500 PASSENGERS

FIFIE The Fifie was a 19th century Scottish fishing boat which was originally an open boat about **30'** (**9 m**) long. However, changing conditions made it necessary for the fishermen to go ever farther out to sea, and so the Fifies were decked over and grew to **70'** (**30 m**). The larger Fifies were lug-rigged with jib and mizzen.

FIFIE HULL

FILE-BOTTOM. see SCHOONER, GLOUCESTER FISHING

FIRESHIP A Fireship was a vessel of little particular value that was filled with combustibles and secured to an enemy ship there to burn both.

In the British Navy a few SHIP-SLOOPS were specifically built to be used as Fireships, and there was a set reward for successful captains and crews of Fireships. Fireships were very successful in defeating the Spanish Armada in **1588**.

FISHING SCHOONER. see SCHOONER, GLOUCESTER FISHING

FIVE-MASTED WOOSUNG JUNK. see JUNK

FLAGSHIP Any ship commanded by a flag officer (see Glossary).

FLATBOAT   A Flatboat was a large, flat-bottomed boat used for landing troops from WARSHIPS in the **18**th and **19**th centuries. Rowed, these boats carried light guns and about **30** men.

FLOATING DOCK   A Floating Dock is constructed of watertight tanks which may be flooded, thus sinking the Dock so that a vessel may enter. The water is then pumped out and the enclosed vessel may be worked on. The advantage of a Floating Dock over a regular dry dock is that it may be towed anywhere.

FLOATING DOCK

TANKS

EMPTY BUT
PARTIALLY FLOODED

SIDE VIEW

FLOODED AND WITH VESSEL FLOATED IN

143

FLOATING INSTRUMENT PLATFORM or FLIP

Flip is a 355' (108.2 m) long vessel which is flipped into vertical position for oceanographic research. She has no motive power of her own and must be towed to the research site. When flipped only 55' (16.7 m) is above water, the remainder consisting of flooded ballast tanks. She is operated by the Scripps Institution of Oceanography at San Diego, California.

Flip BEING TOWED

Flip IN VERTICAL POSITION

FLUTE or **FLUYT**
The Flute was a Dutch MERCHANTMAN, which comprised the bulk of all European commercial shipping at the beginning of the 17th century. In contrast to the PINNACE, which was a little smaller than a full-rigged SHIP of the period, and which was used also for warfare, the Flute was round-sterned.

Due to the system of taxing vessels by their midship bulk, the Flute was built on narrow lines. Since the Flute also carried guns, but on the upper deck only, when more heavily armed vessels removed some of their armaments to make way for more cargo, they were said to be armed 'en flute.'

FLY-BOAT   A Fly-boat was a very high, ornately sterned, flat-bottomed boat with one or two masts used for local Dutch coastal traffic, from the **16**th to the **19**th centuries.

FLYING PRAU.   see PRAHU

FLYING PROA.   see PROA

FREIGHTER.   see CARGO SHIP

FRENCH SHALLOP.   see SHALLOP

FRIENDSHIP SLOOP.   see SLOOP

FRIGATE :

18 TH CENTURY FRIGATE

Frigates, as illustrated opposite, were a class of WARSHIP in all the sailing navies, characterised by relatively little sheer to the hull, and one gun-deck. They were three-masted and ship-rigged, but smaller than the larger SHIPS-OF-THE-LINE, so their duties were not to fight in the line of battle but to act as fast scouts and engage PRIVATEERS.

~ BLACKWALL FRIGATE

Blackwall Frigate was the name applied to a series of trading ships built at Blackwall on the Thames for the Indian trade. They were called Frigates because, in the same way that naval Frigates were finer and faster than SHIPS-OF-THE-LINE, they were finer and faster than the typical EAST INDIAMAN.

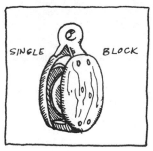

SINGLE BLOCK

~ DESTROYER ESCORT

The modern Frigate, or Destroyer Escort as it is called in the United States, is one of the most all-round types of modern WARSHIP. These ships were developed during World War Two, and originally the American Destroyer Escorts were more strongly armed than the early British Frigates.

U.S. BUCKLEY CLASS DESTROYER ESCORT

Since the Second World War the size of Frigates has increased, as have their functions. Below is a so-called Aircraft Direction Frigate, the British Frigate **Salisbury**.

H.M.S. Salisbury 340' (103 m), 2,180 TONS

~ DONKEY FRIGATE

The Donkey Frigate belonged to a small class of Royal Navy ships built at the end of the 18th and the beginning of the 19th centuries. They carried 28 guns and were really ship-rigged SLOOPS built Frigate-fashion — that is, having a single row of guns protected by the upper deck.

18TH CENT. CANON

THE GALLEON *Griffin*   engraving by VISSCHER

GAIASSA (GYASSI)   The Gyassi is a sailing BARGE, which sails up the Nile, and floats downstream. They range in size from one-masters to three-masters.

GALIZABRA   The Galizabra was a Spanish ship of the 17th and 18th centuries, very similar to a **FRIGATE**, fast, well armed, and a good sailer. The ships were used to bring treasure from the Americas to Spain. By sailing independently they avoided the dangerously slow fleets of **GALLEONS** which were more susceptible to attack.

GALLEASS or **GALLEASSE**   Although the Galleass figured prominently in major engagements of the 15th and 16th centuries, most notably at the battle of Lepanto in 1571, its design as a **WARSHIP** was ultimately abandoned since it suffered the inevitable defects of compromise. Conceived originally as a combination **GALLEY** and **GALLEON**, it could not be rowed as effectively as the **GALLEY** and was not as strong or heavily armed as the **GALLEON**.

By the 17th century the Galleass was used as a trading vessel for long voyages, from Genoa to Denmark for example. A single bank of oars augmented the three lateen-rigged masts, but the rams of the early Galleasses had disappeared.

RAM

TYPE OF GALLEASS USED AT LEPANTO

GALLEON   There are several theories about the origin of the Galleon, but it seems to have been an English development of the **CARRACK**, following Sir John Hawkins's experiments in eliminating the high forecastles of contemporary ships, which made it very hard to sail to windward. This took place in **1570**. Within **20** years the Galleon had been established in Spain, although the name was never used in England or northern Europe. Originally a **WARSHIP**, the Galleon became the principle trading ship of the time.

16 TH CENTURY GALLEON

GALLEY: The simplest definition of a Galley is of a ship with one deck, propelled by oars, and usually used for fighting. However, since Galleys were used from about **3,000** B.C. to as late as the Russo-Swedish war of **1809**, it will be appreciated that there have been many, many types.

Probably originating with the Egyptians, the Galley was used and developed by the Phoenicians, from which the Greeks developed the **BIREME** and the **TRIREME**; these in turn evolved, with the Carthaginians and the Romans, into larger, multi-banked, vessels, until finally the single-decked Galley again supplanted the earlier models. Mainly because of its speed, the Galley remained a pre-eminent fighting vessel for many centuries.

Much used by Mediterranian pirates, the Galley was not much good in heavy weather, and with advances in speed and seaworthiness of other vessels, the Galley finally disappeared in the late 18th century.

17TH CENTURY GALLEY

~ CONTINENTAL GALLEY

The Continental Galley was a light craft used in the American Revolutionary War, fitted for rowing - hence the name Galley - and variously rigged as CUTTER, SLOOP, or SCHOONER.

Anything from 40' (12 m) to 75' (22 m) in length, they carried from one to twelve guns. After the War they were used in the West Indies until about 1825.

CONTINENTAL GALLEY 1776

~PENTECONTER

The Penteconter is typical of the larger Greek Galleys, having twenty-five oars to a side. Greek and Roman Galleys were classified according to how many oars, how many banks of oars, and how many men at each oar exist. The classifications are often argued about; all we know for certain are some of the names, for example BIREMES (supposedly with two banks), TRIREMES (with three banks), and so on up to QUINQUEREME, (supposedly with five banks – which would seem to be impossible), and even more. A TRIREME with a total of twenty-five oars on the thranite (upper), zygite (middle), and thalamite (lower) banks was known as a Penteconter.

GREEK PENTECONTER 1000 B.C.

GALLIOT   The Galliot was originally a small **GALLEY** with sixteen or twenty oars and a single mast, used to chase and board enemy ships in the 17th and 18th centuries.

During the 18th century it became the accepted term for a Dutch vessel used in coastal traffic, much like British **BARGES**.

GALWAY HOOKER   The Galway Hooker was actually a **CUTTER**-rigged fishing boat originating in Galway, Ireland, and introduced to New England around **1857**.

GARUKHA.   see DHOW

GARVEY   The Garvey is one of the oldest native American boats, reputed, in fact, to have been one of the first boats used in New Jersey. Similar to the scow, the Garvey is a small sailing workboat.

SPRITSAIL

SPRIT

CENTERBOARD

GEHAZI.   see DHOW

GELLYWATTE   Gellywatte is a very old word for the boat used by a ship's captain when he went ashore, and is thought to be the origin of the term JOLLYBOAT.

GHOBUN   The Ghobun is a native dugout CANOE with an outrigger as long as the hull. The Ghobun comes from the Astrolabe Bay District of Papua New Guinea.

Two small mat sails are carried from a two-storied platform, and high washstrakes give the Ghobun much freeboard.

MAT SAILS

PLATFORMS

CARVED WASHSTRAKE

OUTRIGGER

GIG   A Gig was a narrow, light, ship's boat, generally rowed with four or six oars but also often equipped with two short masts.

GUNTER-RIGGED GIG

GIGLIO TRAWLER.   see TRAWLER

GLOUCESTER FISHING SCHOONER.   see SCHOONER

GONDOLA

a.   Benedict Arnold had a number of 'Gondolas' built on Lake Erie, and with them held up the British for a year during the American Revolution, but they should have been called GUNDALOWS.

b.   A Gondola is a small Italian passenger boat, rowed with six or eight oars, used on the coast.

c.   The best-known Gondola is the light pleasure boat used on the canals in Venice, Italy. The Gondola is mentioned as early as **1094**, but its hull form is remarkably modern, conforming to modern wave-line theory.

The best-known feature of the Gondola is the metal ferro in the shape of the ancient 'rostrum tridens,' which surmounts the high stem.

TRADITIONAL
GONDOLA BEAK
(FERRO)

GOPHER.   see GUFA

GRAB   The Grab was an Indian coasting vessel of the 18th and 19th centuries. Lateen-rigged, the larger Grabs had two masts, the smaller Grabs a single mast, augmented by sweeps for rowing.

GREAT LAKES SCHOONER.   see SCHOONER

GREEK MERCHANT SHIP.   see MERCHANTMEN

GUARD-SHIP   Although the chief meaning of Guard-ship is that of the ship so stationed at a port to act as guard for the rest of the fleet, there have been other meanings. The Guard-ship was usually the FLAGSHIP of the Port Admiral; the ship to which men obtained by press gangs were first brought; the boat which makes the round of the fleet at night.

GUFA (GOPHER)   The Gufa (also spelled Gufah) is a CORACLE-type of craft used on the River Tigris. It is made of dried reeds coated with bitumen, and may have been the craft referred to in the Bible when Noah was instructed to "build an ARK of gopher wood."

الع[ا]راق

GUL   The Gul is a peculiar outrigger DUGOUT sailing CANOE from the Islands that lie in Torres Straits between Queensland, Australia and Papua New Guinea. Sometimes as long as **50' (15m)** to **60' (18m)** the sails, made of matting, were originally two high oblongs. Nowadays, Western fore-and-aft sails are used.

GUNBOAT :   Gunboats were first used in the U.S. Navy during the war of **1812**. Rigged as SLOOPS, CUTTERS, SCHOONERS, and some as lateen-rigged vessels, they were quite small — about **50' (15m)** — and carried a **24-** or **32** pounder and a small carronade.

U.S. GUNBOAT, 1803

161

~ MOTOR GUNBOAT (M.G.B.)

By the 20th century most countries had built small, heavily armed vessels for coastal defence, which were mostly called Gunboats but which were, in reality, small CRUISERS.

During the Second World War, several navies built very fast, small WARSHIPS designed for anti-shipping patrols in coastal waters. Those built for the British Navy were known as M.G.B.'s, and could make 40 knots.

SWEDISH MOTOR GUNBOAT, 1870

BRITISH COASTAL DEFENCE BOAT 1945

162

GUNDALOW or **GUNDELO**   Sometimes known as a Merrimac Gundalow, the Gundalow was a river **BARGE** used on the Merrimac and other New England rivers in the 18th century.

The Gundalow was unusual in having a short-masted lateen-rigged sail with the main yard weighted before the mast with a counter-balance.

COUNTERBALANCE

MERRIMAC GUNDALOW

GYASSI.   see GAIASSA

A MERCHANT SHIP

19TH Century British woodcut

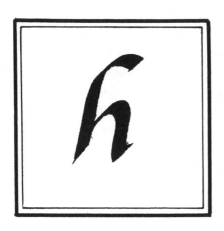

HAAK   The Haak is a large Dutch sailing LIGHTER, averaging 120′ (36.5 m) long.   There is considerable sheer at the bow and stern, and very little free-board amidships.

HAGBOAT

Hagboat was the term used to describe a type of 18th century MERCHANTMAN distinguished from a PINK and a FRIGATE by the hull planking continuing around the stern and finishing under the taffrail, and distinguished from a CAT and a BARQUE by its beakhead. It must be remembered that at this time any of the above vessels could be rigged various ways, and so the easiest way to define a vessel was by the hull type. Nowadays, most of the above names refer to specific rigs, and so vessels may be classified by rig rather than by hull type.

STERN OF FRIGATE — TAFFRAIL — SQUARE STERN — ROUND STERN — STERN OF HAGBOAT

BOW OF CAT AND BARQUE — BEAKHEAD — BOW OF HAGBOAT

HALF-CLIPPER.   see CLIPPER

HATCH-BOAT   A Hatch-boat was quite simply a boat whose deck was covered with hatches. Used on the lower Thames in the **18**th and **19**th centuries, spritsails were the first rig, but were later supplanted by gaff mainsails, with no boom'. Bigger Hatch-boats had double topsails and a mizzen mast.

GAFF MAINSAIL

HAVRE PILOT BOAT.   see PILOT BOAT

HAVRE TRAWLER.   see TRAWLER

HAY BARGE.   see BARGE

BOATSWAIN'S CALL

HEMMEMA The Hemmema was one of the last swedish attempts at a combination GALLEY and sailing MAN-OF-WAR. Built towards the end of the 18th century, the Hemmema was like a twenty-six gun FRIGATE with pairs of oars between her guns.

HERMAPHRODITE BRIG. see BRIG

HIGH-CHARGED SHIP A High-charged ship was a WARSHIP of the period before 1585 when vessels were built with high castles in the bow (forecastles) and stern (sterncastles), from which the archers and musketeers assailed the enemy. See also LOW-CHARGED SHIPS.

HOGGIE A Hoggie was a British fishing craft from the Channel port of Brighton. Popular until about 1850, it was flat, round-ended, and of great beam.

BRIGHTON HOGGIE 1800

HONG KONG CARGO JUNK.   see JUNK

HOOGAAR   The Hoogar is a CUTTER-rigged Dutch pleasure boat, with great forward sheer, a long bowsprit, and deep leeboards.

HOOKER   Hooker is a slightly contemptuous term for a vessel past her prime, but originally referred to a fishing vessel (which fished with hooks on a long line) developed from the KETCH.

HOOKER 1775

169

HOPPER   Hoppers are **LIGHTERS** with no means of self-propulsion, which are towed behind **DREDGERS** to receive, and then carry away and dump, that which is dredged up.

HORNBAEK BOAT   Used for plaice fishing from Hornbaek, the Danish Hornbaek Boat is **CUTTER**-rigged and carries a yard topsail from a single pole mast.

HOUARIO   The Houario was a two-masted Mediterranean pleasure boat of the 18th century. The sails were set with sliding topmasts.

SLIDING TOPMASTS

HOUSEBOAT In various parts of the world people live not in houses but on boats, whose function is mainly that of a dwelling rather than of a vessel. Such colonies of boat dwellers are to be found in the crowded port cities of the East, such as Singapore and Hong Kong, on the lakes of Kashmir, and in more affluent societies of the West.

Some Western houseboats are specifically designed as such, and can often travel, usually with an engine, but many more are often little more than old vessels, permanently moored or half-grounded, such as old **BARGES**.

AN EXPENSIVE WESTERN HOUSEBOAT

HOVERCRAFT

Although the principle of the Hovercraft was first considered in **1875**, it wasn't until **1950** that the first practical design was evolved by Sir Christopher Cockerell, and **1968** that the first vessel went into service (as a cross-channel **FERRY**).

The Hovercraft is propelled forward by four large air screws while resting on a cushion of air produced by fans under the hull. This cushion of air is retained by a **7'(2.1m)** neoprene skirt which enables the vessel to ride not only over land but over water and waves up to **5'(1.5m)** high.

AIR SCREWS

NEOPRENE SKIRT

HOWKER

The Howker was a round-sterned **MERCHANTMAN** used in Northern Europe during the **17**th and **18**th centuries, related to the **BUSS** and **DOGGER**.

HOY

a.   The sailing LIGHTERS of the East India Company were known as Hoys.

b.   The TENDERS used in the British Navy from 1700 to 1740 were known as Hoys.

c.   Hoy was also the word most commonly used for any small coasting vessel of the 16th, 17th, 18th centuries. Usually single-masted but with a variety of rigs, the Hoy was also variously known as a SMACK or SLOOP.

17TH CENTURY HOY

HUDSON RIVER SLOOP.   SEE SLOOP

HULK

a.   The Hulk was originally a large CARGO SHIP contemporary with the CARRACK. It then came to mean any large, unwieldy ship with rounded bows and stern.

16TH CENTURY HULK

b.   Until the end of the 18th century, the word Hulk was also used to denote the hull of a ship.

c.   The present-day meaning of Hulk is of an old ship converted to some use which does not require it to move, such as a floating storehouse. Hulks as such were often used to step and remove masts in and from other ships. It was because of overcrowding in Thames Hulks in 1776 (used as prisons), that Australia was in part colonized as a penal settlement.

HUMBER KEEL.   see KEEL

HVALOR PILOT BOAT.   see PILOT BOAT

HYDROFOIL   A Hydrofoil has foils fitted beneath the hull which lift the vessel clear of the water when traveling at high speed; when not, the vessel floats as other craft.

There are now two basic types of Hydrofoils: those that ride on a cushion of air, clear of the water (except for the propelling screw), and those that have the forward foil (there are generally two, one forward and one aft) partially submerged, which decreases the speed but increases the stability.

HYLAM JUNK.   see JUNK

A PASSENGER VESSEL   early 20th century French engraving

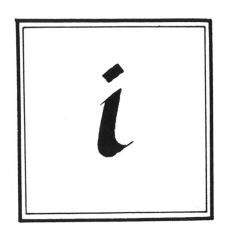

ICEBOAT.   see YACHT

ICEBREAKER   An icebreaker is a vessel specially designed, with strong bow and engines, to break a path through ice for merchant shipping.

FORWARD SCREWS FOR PUSHING ICE AFT

ICE

ICE YACHT.   see YACHT

INBOARD MOTORBOAT.   see MOTORBOAT

INBOARD RACER.   see MOTORBOAT

INDIAN CANOES.   see CANOE

INDIAN-HEADER.   see SCHOONER, GLOUCESTER FISHING

INTERNATIONAL DRAGON CLASS.   see YACHT, RACING

IRISH WICKER VESSEL   Certainly related to the **CURRAGH**, the Irish Wicker Vessel shown below (from a drawing made about **1670**) had not changed much since the Roman Invasion of Britain, when similar boats were described by Latin authors.

OX SKULL

KILLICK (STONE AND WOOD ANCHOR)

IRONCLAD

After the Crimean War it was realized that the age of wooden SHIPS-OF-THE-LINE was over, in part due to increased armaments and in part due to the obvious fact that metal-protected hulls lasted longer against such powerful fire.

Thus the first Ironclads were built — France built the **Gloire** in **1859**, Britain built **H.M.S. Warrior** in **1860** — which had armour plating covering part or all of their sides.

The name Ironclad remained the generic term for all iron or steel WARSHIPS until the advent of **H.M.S. Dreadnought** in **1906**, from which date subsequent WARSHIPS were known as DREADNOUGHTS.

Gloire : 1859

Tsesarevitch : 1901

ISE FJORD FISHING BOAT

The Ise Fjord Fishing Boat, from Denmark, is similar to the HORNBAEK BOAT, but in general has a shallower and beamier hull.

ITALIAN LATEENER

The Italian Lateener was really the Mediterranean counterpart of the northern YAWL, with a square topsail.

JACHT The word **YACHT** comes from Jacht, which was a small Dutch fast sailing boat. Originally used for state purposes, like **ESNECCAS**, they became **DISPATCH BOATS**.

DUTCH JACHT 1660

JACKASS - BARQUE .   see BARQUENTINE

JACKASS - SCHOONER .   see SCHOONER

JAEGT   The Jaegt , a Norwegian craft in use from the 14th to the 19th century, was the direct descendant of the **VIKING** LONGSHIP. Used mainly for coastwise trade, it was also used for traditional wedding parties .

JAPANESE JUNK . see JUNK

JAVANESE PRAU (PRAO) .   see PRAHU

J-CLASS YACHT .   see YACHT, RACING

JOLLY-BOAT The Jolly-Boat, usually carried in davits over the stern, was a general purpose ship's boat used for such things as rowing round the ship to see that the yards were square. It may be derived from YAWL or GELLYWATTE.

JUNK : The word Junk comes from the Portuguese, 'junco,' adapted from the Javanese word for ship, 'djong.' Junk is the name applied to a wide variety of Eastern sailing vessels characterized by flat bottoms, square bows, and high sterns. The typical Junk sail is essentially a lugsail stiffened with horizontal battens.

~ AMOY JUNK The Amoy Junk is one of the more typical South China Junks, although these sometimes show more Western influence, and carry jibs for example.

BATTENS

EYE PAINTED ON BOW

~CHINESE JUNK
about 1825.

The Chinese Junk shown below is from a drawing made in

The Foochow Stock Junk, similar to the vessel shown above, and so called because it chiefly carried timber from Pei Ho in the north to Canton in the south, is the Junk which is usually sold as a model to tourists as the typical Chinese Junk.

~ FIVE-MASTED WOOSUNG JUNK

~ HONG KONG CARGO JUNK

~HYLAM JUNK

The Hylam Junk was once common in the Gulf of Siam Trade.

90' (27.5m) LENGTH

~JAPANESE JUNK

~ MALAY EAST COASTER

~ NORTH CHINA JUNK

~ **SINGAPORE JUNK**

~ **TWAKO** or **TWAQO**   The Twako comes from Singapore,
and has the typical Chinese
battened lugsail and flat-bottomed keel, so is also a Junk.

~ WEST RIVER CHINESE JUNK

ADMIRAL RODNEY DEFEATING THE FRENCH AT THE BATTLE OF THE SAINTS, 1782
contemporary British woodcut

KAEP.   see PROA

KAIKI   The Kaiki is a small, lateen-rigged boat from Greece. A jib is sometimes carried on a sharply steeved bowsprit and there is no rudder, the boat being steered with an oar or a paddle.

KAUPSKIP   Kaupskip was the general name for the Norse vessels which made the expeditions to Iceland, Greenland, and Vinland (America) in the **10**th and **11**th centuries. Kaupskip actually means trading ship, for that is what these vessels normally were. Unlike the **VIKING** LONGSHIPS they had keels, but were otherwise similar, with square sails, oars and no deck.

KAYAK   Kayak is an Eskimo word for a light **CANOE** made of skins stretched over a wooden frame. The occupant laces himself into a hole in the center of the top of the boat to ensure watertightness. Kayaks are always one-man boats; if a woman, or more than one person uses a similar **CANOE** it is called an **UMIAK**.

KEEL :   The Keel is a flat-bottomed sailing **BARGE** once used extensively in north-east England for loading **COLLIERS** before modern mechanical methods were developed.

~ HUMBER KEEL   The Humber Keel, shown opposite, was the Keel most typical to the Humber River. Leeboards were used when sailing at sea.

HUMBER KEEL

~TYNE KEEL

The Tyne Keel was also a coal-carrying sailing **BARGE**, very similar to the MERSEY **LIGHTER**.

KETCH :
The Ketch was originally a small ship with no foremast (ships proper having three masts) used for coastal trading from the 17th century on.

17 TH CENTURY KETCH

Modern ketches are fore-and-aft rigged; and since the mizzen mast is always stepped forward of the steering gear this has come to be accepted as the definition of ketch, at least in comparison to the modern **YAWL**, whose mizzen mast is always stepped abaft the steering gear, but actually it is the relative sizes of the sails which is the determining factor.

TWO MASTS :

MIZZEN = $\frac{1}{3}$ MAIN (AREA)

(YAWL HAS TWO MASTS, BUT MIZZEN = $\frac{1}{4}$ OR LESS THAN MAIN)

MODERN KETCH

~ BOMB KETCH

Since the 18th century ketch had only two masts, mortars were mounted just forward of the mainmast, with which to bombard the enemy — which gives rise to the theory that the ketch was really a three-masted vessel with the foremast removed so that the mortar could fire unobstructedly. In fact, the two-masted ketch existed before mortars, and was used for carrying messages because of its ability to sail in almost any wind.

MORTAR

MORTAR   MAINMAST   MIZZEN MAST

ENGLISH BOMB KETCH 1688

~ LAKE MICHIGAN KETCH

Concurrent with their naval use, ketches were always used commercially. Some think that the very name comes from their having been used as fishing boats. They were also used for general cargo, as was the Lake Michigan Ketch, which carried lumber on the Great Lakes.

KLIPPER   A Klipper is a Dutch vessel used for cargo, about **65'** (**19.8m**) to **80'** (**24m**) long. Today all Klippers are steel built with diesel engines; they were formerly rigged as **KETCHES** and used leeboards.

KNOCKABOUT.   see SCHOONER, GLOUCESTER FISHING

KNORR.   see VIKING SHIP

KOFF   A Koff is a Dutch working boat of considerable age, having changed considerably over the past 200 years. Originally rigged like a **GALLIOT**, some **18**th century Koffs carried spritsails rigged either **KETCH** or **SCHOONER** fashion.

18 TH CENTURY
KOFF

19 TH CENTURY
KOFF

KOLEH   The Koleh is a Malay racing CANOE. They are reputedly very fast but suffer from an inability to come about with ease.

KOTIA.   see DHOW

KURRAN KAHN   The Kurran Kahn is a small open trawl-fishing boat from Lithuania.

SPRIT MAINSAIL

JIB

SPRIT FORESAIL

THE EXPLOSION OF *L'Orient* AT THE BATTLE OF THE NILE, 1798
contemporary British woodcut

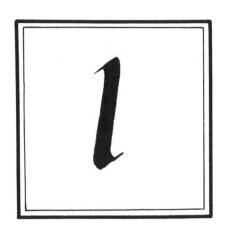

LACCADIVE ISLANDS CANOE.   see CANOE

LAKATOI   The Lakatoi is a large sailing **RAFT** from Papua New Guinea, consisting of several logs, side-by-side, held together by a large platform.

LAKE MICHIGAN KETCH. see KETCH

LANCHANG   A Lanchang is a Malay seagoing craft with two equal lugsails. Although the type varies somewhat from place to place, overhanging bows and sterns are common.

LANDING CRAFT   For the large amphibious operations undertaken during the Second World War, a number of specialized vessels were built to deliver men and materiel on the beaches. Some of these Landing Craft are described below.

a.   L.C.A.   Landing Craft Assaults were small landing craft used for marine assaults on enemy beaches during the Second World War.

b.   L.C.I.   Landing Craft Infantry were small craft designed to carry infantry ashore. L.C.I.'s were normally carried in davits on L.S.I.'s until needed. The L.C.I.'s had bow doors which were opened when the craft grounded.

c.   L.C.P.   Landing Craft Personnel were small wooden Landing Craft used for transporting personnel on assault operations.

d.   L.C.S.   Landing Craft Support were small Landing Craft which carried Oerlikon guns and were used as supporting vessels during landing assaults.

e.   L.C.T.   Landing Craft, Tank were the vessels which carried the tanks from L.C.S.'s ashore. Small L.C.T.'s were carried at the davits of L.C.S.'s, but there were also larger, self-propelled L.C.T.'s, such as the French one shown below.

f.   L.C.U.   Landing Craft Utility were also armed personnel carriers with bow doors for beach unloading.

OPENING ARC OF BOW DOOR

g. L.S.I. Landing Ship, Infantry were large ships converted for carrying and landing infantry, either from boats carried at their davits (L.C.I.'s), or through bow doors, if they could be beached.

h. L.S.M. Landing Ship Medium carried personnel and materiel, landed through bow doors.

BOW DOORS

i. L.S.T. Landing Ship, Tank was a large merchant ship converted to carry **700** troops and **20** amphibious tanks. These large vessels could be grounded, but also carried smaller Landing Craft against unfavorable conditions.

LAPIL or **LEPALEPA** . see CANOE

LAUNCH

a. During the 18th and 19th centuries, Launch was the name given to a flat-bottomed open GUNBOAT used by the navies of France. Spain, the Italian states, and Turkey.

b. The word Launcha, which is thought to be of Malay origin, came into English from Spanish, and gradually replaced the word SHALLOP. Launch (or SHALLOP) was another term for the largest ship's boat carried on a British MAN-OF-WAR.

c. Nowadays Launch is the generic name for the small power boat used as a TENDER for pleasure YACHTS. Larger YACHTS often carry a Launch on board.

LIBERTY SHIP. see CARGO SHIP

LIFEBOAT A Lifeboat meant at first (when Lifeboat stations were established in England in **1823**), a small open boat especially designed for seaworthiness in heavy weather.

Nowadays, modern Lifeboats are motor-driven vessels fitted with radio and all manner of life-saving equipment.

OLD ROWING LIFEBOAT

MODERN MOTOR LIFEBOAT

204

LIFERAFT   A Liferaft was originally a raft made on board, of any available wood, to save life in a calamity, but nowadays many ships carry inflatable rubber Liferafts for the same purpose

LIGHTER: A Lighter is strictly a DUMB VESSEL, i.e. one with no means of self-propulsion, used for carrying freight from ship to shore and vice-versa.

~ MERSEY LIGHTER   The Mersey Lighter is actually a SAILING BARGE, similar to the KEEL, but is used as a Lighter - to unlade ships.

205

~ RANGOON LIGHTER

The Rangoon Lighter is even less a Lighter than the MERSEY LIGHTER since it is used as a CARGO SHIP in its own right. Built entirely of teak, this Indian vessel does, nonetheless, somewhat resemble the MERSEY LIGHTER.

LIGHTSHIP

A Lightship's function is that of a lighthouse; to warn shipping of shoal water or hidden obstruction, usually at a location where it would be impracticable to build a lighthouse. Usually painted red, they are being replaced by Lanby* buoys.
* (Large Automatic Navigational Buoy)

LIGHT

LINER.   see PASSENGER SHIP

LISI.   see CANOE

LONGBOAT   The Longboat was the largest of the ship's boats carried on **18**th century **WARSHIPS**, and was the boat from which the **LAUNCH** was developed. One of its main purposes was to fetch water, another was to be the principal **LIFEBOAT**, hence it was rigged and kept provisioned.

ROYAL NAVY LONGBOAT 1730

LONGSHIP.   see VIKING SHIP

LORCHA The Lorcha is said to have been originated by the Portuguese when they first settled Macao. It has a Western hull, but carries a Chinese JUNK rig.

LOUISIANA PIROGUE. SEE PIROGUE

LOW-CHARGED SHIPS When the high forecastles were abandoned on 16th century WARSHIPS, they became known as Low-charged Ships in contradistinction to the earlier HIGH-CHARGED SHIPS.

LOWESTOFT SMACK .   see SMACK

LOWESTOFT TRAWLER .   see TRAWLER

LUGGER :   A Lugger is a sailing vessel, usually two-masted, rigged with lugsails. The lug rig became popular towards the end of the 17th century, particularly for fishing boats and other coastwise craft, due to the ease of handling compared to the square sail.

~ BELGIAN LUGGER   The Belgian Lugger was a fishing boat with two lugsails and a smaller triangular sail set on a mizzen mast.

KILLICK

PRIMITIVE STONE
ANCHOR

~ DEAL LUGGER

The Deal Lugger was a very old boat which originally carried three lugsails, but which later discarded the mainmast. The Deal Lugger was used by pilots and for life-saving as well as 'hovelling,' which meant looking for hauling and salvage jobs.

DEAL LUGGER 1870

~ DOUARNENEZ LUGGER

The Douarnenez Lugger, from Brittany, was one of the last commercial sailing fishing boats.

~ ETAPLES LUGGER

The Etaples Lugger was a French fishing boat, with a main lug, and mizzen lug which often carried a lug topsail.

~ MORBIHAN LUGGER

The Morbihan Lugger was a Breton fishing boat with curiously tall sails; it was, however, a very fast boat.

~ MOUSEHOLE LUGGER

Mousehole is a port in Cornwall, England, whence came the Mousehole Lugger, a three-master, complete with topsails and jib.

MOUSEHOLE LUGGER 1840

~ NEW ORLEANS LUGGER

used in the Gulf of Mexico, the New Orleans Lugger, a single-master, was of European origin.

~ YORKSHIRE LUGGER

fishing boat used off the east coast of England.

The Yorkshire Lugger, now extinct, was a beamy

YORKSHIRE LUGGER 1815

AN EARLY 19TH CENTURY BRIG-SLOOP   19th century British woodcut

MACSHIP Macships, whose name comes from the initial letters of Merchant Aircraft Carrier, were **TANKERS** or similar merchant shipping fitted with a temporary flight deck. This was to enable land-based aircraft to land and take off, thus providing protection from the long-range German Focke-Wulf aircraft. When these attacks ceased, Macships were used to fight submarines by carrying aircraft armed with depth charges.

MADURA PRAU. see PRAHU

MAIN TOPSAIL SCHOONER. see SCHOONER

MALAR PANSHI

The Malar Panshi is a primitive sailing DUGOUT from Bengal, to which a high steering platform has been added.

MALAY EAST COASTER.   see JUNK

MALAY OUTRIGGER CANOE.   see CANOE

MALDIVE ISLANDS TRADER

The Maldive Islands lie in the Indian Ocean, south-west of India, and are the home of this large, three-masted trading vessel, known as a Maldive Islands Trader.

Many features reminiscent of the 15th century, such as the hull shape, lateen mizzen, poop, and overhanging forecastle provoke interesting speculation as to this vessel's provenance.

MALDIVE ISLAND TRADER

MAN-OF-WAR .   see WARSHIP

MAN-OF-WAR BRIG   see BRIG

MAORI WAR CANOE .   see CANOE

MARKAB   The Markab is a **DHOW**-like Egyptian boat.

MASHVA or **MASHWA**.   see MUCHVA

MAST SHIP   A Mast ship was a vessel used for the
                      transporting of mast timber, in the days
of sail. Such long timber necessitated large ports cut in the
bows and stern.   Mast ships carried on extensive trade with
the Baltic countries, where suitable trees grew, and also, later,
with North America.

MASTLESS SHIP   Mastless ship was the term by which
                          the first BATTLESHIPS to rely entirely
on steam propulsion were known.

MERCHANTMEN :   Merchantmen is the term used to
                          refer to all commercial vessels.
However, although all types of WARSHIPS and pleasure boats
privately owned are excluded, the term also usually excludes
special-purpose vessels which are neither naval nor private
but commercial, and generally refers to cargo-carrying,
trading vessels, more specifically from the days of sail;
modern Merchantmen being referred to as vessels of the
Merchant Marine.

        As with WARSHIPS, it was the Phoenicians who developed
the first purely merchant ship from earlier Egyptian models.

PHOENICIAN TIMBER SHIP, FROM AN ASSYRIAN SCULPTURE
700 B.C.

218

After the Phoenicians, the Greeks and the Romans became the great sea powers. It was at this time that a firm distinction was made between **WARSHIPS** and Merchantmen. The fighting ship was moved by oars but the Merchantman depended on sails. Also, **GALLEYS**, which were built for speed, were long and thin, whereas Merchantmen were short and fat.

GOOSE HEAD

ROMAN MERCHANTMAN
200 A.D.

In the same way that many Phoenician ships had horse's heads as figureheads, many Roman Merchant ships had goose heads carved in the stern.

see also **ROMAN TRADER**.

For many centuries after the demise of the Roman Empire, time spent on a voyage was of less economic importance than bulk of cargo. Therefore Merchantmen continued to be beamier and slower than contemporary WARSHIPS. Also, because the large crews used to work WARSHIPS could not be afforded by traders, rigging tended to be simpler and easier to work.

Until about **1500** the average Merchantman could be typified by the CARAVEL, of up to **250** tons.

With the discovery of the New World in the 15th century, Merchant shipping increased in size and design, and so after **1500** it is the CARRACK which best exemplifies medieval merchant ships.

SPANISH CARAVEL
250 TONS, 1490

(NOTE: THESE TWO SHIPS
ARE NOT TO THE SAME SCALE)

ENGLISH CARRACK
1,600 TONS, 1520

As the discovery of the New World had given an impetus to merchant shipping design, so did the advent of trade with the Orient stimulate development even further.

Many countries formed East India Companies and built larger ships to take advantage of this great new trade. These Merchantmen were called EAST INDIAMEN. They grew steadily in size until eventually they often outstripped WARSHIPS, often carrying guns to defend themselves.

EAST INDIAMAN , MID-1700's

As trade continued to grow in the **17**th, **18**th, and **19**th centuries the merchant ship evolved into a faster vessel since speed became an important factor in the increased competition. Ships grew longer in relation to their beam, and ever more sail was crowded on.

Even the introduction of steam did little to diminish the profitability of the big **CLIPPER SHIPS** since not enough coal could be carried for the long eastern voyages.

When the Suez Canal was opened in **1869**, the China tea trade and the Australian wool trade finally fell into the hands of the steamers.

Similarly, the nitrate trade from South America remained with the great four-masted **BARQUES** and five-masted **SCHOONERS** until the opening of the Panama Canal in **1914** made the route short enough for steamers.

AMERICAN CLIPPER BARQUE
1870

Merchantmen made the transition to steam faster than WARSHIPS since the vulnerability of paddle wheels to gunfire was not a risk.

By **1900** most of the passenger-carrying trade was done by steam and the trend towards ever bigger ships continued until air travel rendered most sea travel (except for pleasure) unviable.

Merchant shipping however has increased dramatically. In **1945** the largest merchant vessels were around **50,000** tons. By **1975** there were vessels of over **300,000** tons!

SCHOONER-RIGGED STEAMER
CARGO SHIP, 1881

THE NINETEENTH CENTURY MERCHANTMAN
IN TRANSITION

Once again in the history of Merchantmen speed is no longer the prime consideration. No ship is faster than an airplane, and with the advent of refrigeration that which travels by sea does so because that is the most economical way to move bulk, not because it is the fastest way.

Consequently a large proportion of today's 'Merchantmen' uses diesel propulsion, and in other fields diesel has replaced the steam engine, although it is to be expected that sooner or later, nuclear power, which at present is reserved for naval use, will be developed for use by the merchant fleets of the world, possibly in conjunction with a modernized return to sail, as with the German DYNASHIP.

TURRET DECK CARGO
BOAT, 1917

MERGUI PEARLER   The Mergui Pearler comes from the Mergui Archipelago in the Indian Ocean near Burma. Lug-rigged, the Mergui Pearler has definite Malayan characteristics.

MERSEY LIGHTER.   see LIGHTER

METER CLASS YACHT.   see YACHT, RACING

M.G.B.   see GUNBOAT, MOTOR

MIDGET SUBMARINE.   see SUBMARINE

SAIL

MARLING HITCH

MINELAYER

Mines were first used during the Crimean War **1854-1856**, and since that time many different vessels have served as Minelayers. Shown below is a British ship of **1,000** tons designed specifically as a coastal Minelayer.

BRITISH MINELAYER

MINESWEEPER

Minelayers of course produced Mine-sweepers, originally two vessels to a sweep. But now there are many different kinds, such as Deep-sea Sweepers, Coastal Sweepers, and Harbor Sweepers. Shown below is a U.S. Coastal Minesweeper much used by NATO countries.

AMERICAN BLUEBIRD CLASS MINESWEEPER

226

MOLETTA   The Moletta was a fishing boat of the Tagus River, Portugal, and which, when the weather was favorable, hoisted all sorts of jib-shaped sails around the main lateen sail.

MOLICEIRO   The Moliceiro is a lug-rigged Portuguese boat with a remarkably curved prow and a rounded stern.

FLAT BOTTOM

227

MON.   see CANOE

MONITOR   The Monitor was a very low freeboard and shallow-draught ship carrying one or two large guns designed for coastal bombardment. Used extensively by the British Navy in World War I, they have now been rendered obsolete by guided missiles

The original ship, the **Monitor**, was designed by John Ericsson for the Union Navy during the American Civil War.

Monitor : 1862

MORBIHAN LUGGER.   see LUGGER

MOTORBOAT :   Although nowadays the vast majority of all craft over 20' (7m) have engines, even if they are only auxiliary engines, the term Motorboat applies only to those where the engine is the main motive source, and which are generally small and used for pleasure purposes.

Originally, a small, open boat fitted with either an inboard or outboard engine was known as a Motorboat, but the type has grown, as the following examples show, so that it is hard to apply a strict definition — not every boat with a motor may be a Motorboat!

~ CABIN CRUISER

A cabin cruiser may be any size from very small to very large — although the more opulent ones over **50'** (**16m**) tend to be called MOTOR YACHTS. MOTOR YACHTS are usually seagoing, whereas cabin cruisers are generally only used on inland waters.

~ INBOARD MOTORBOAT

Inboard Motorboat implies that the engine is fixed, and built into the boat, the only part outside the boat being the screw, or screws.

INBOARD MOTORBOAT

~ INBOARD RACER

Inboard Racers are very powerful Motorboats that often engage in lengthy offshore racers at speeds of more than 100 m.p.h. (160 m.).

~ OUTBOARD MOTORBOAT

Outboard Motorboats are usually small open, or semi-decked boats with outboard motors which are usually mounted on the transom as shown below.

OUTBOARD

The kind of Motorboat shown above is often known as a Runabout, used as a small utility boat.

~ OUTBOARD RACER

Built for speed, the Outboard Racer is a streamlined craft with a high-power outboard engine.

~ SPORT FISHERMAN

Sport Fishermen are often luxurious, high-powered Motorboats designed for deep-sea fishing. High observation decks for sighting the fish often give these boats a top-heavy look.

MOTOR SAILER

Motor Sailers are usually cruising pleasure boats, often KETCH-rigged, but having substantial engines, so that the boat is equally designed for power and sail.

In the early days of power, before the majority of commercial fishing craft were powered by engine alone, many could have been called Motor Sailers, having both engines and sails, although, in general, the term is reserved for pleasure boats.

MOTOR SAILER UNDER SAIL

MOTOR TORPEDO BOAT.   SEE TORPEDO BOAT

MOTOR TRAWLER.   see TRAWLER

MOTOR YACHT.   see YACHT

MOUSEHOLE LUGGER.   see LUGGER

MOUNT'S BAY DRIVER   The Mount's Bay Driver was a Cornish fishing boat, KETCH-rigged, but with no bowsprit. The mainsail was usually a lugsail while the mizzen was gaff-rigged and often carried a topsail.

M.T.B.   see TORPEDO BOAT

MTEPI.   see CANOE

MUCHVA (MASHVA)

Muchva is a word used on the East African coast and other places on the Indian Ocean for small boats in general. Large DHOWS often carry Muchvas on board. Elsewhere they are used as transport and fishing vessels.

MULETTA

The Muletta was a Portuguese fishing boat closely related to the MOLETTA.

MULTI-HULL

A Multi-Hull is any craft with two or more hulls, whether it be propelled by sail or power. CATAMARANS are multi-hulls which have two identical hulls. TRIMARANS are multi-hulls which have a central hull and two floats. While relatively new in the occident, Multi-hulls have been used for hundreds of years in the Indian and Pacific oceans.

MONO HULL   MULTI-HULLS

CATAMARAN   TRIMARAN

MUMBLE - BEE

Mumble-bees were beamy CUTTER-rigged TRAWLERS once common off the south coast of England.

A 19TH CENTURY FRENCH FRIGATE   19th century British woodcut

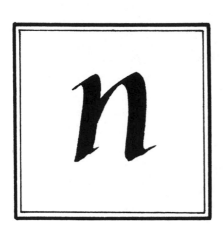

NABBY
The Nabby, a sailing SKIFF from the west coast of Scotland, is a double-ended, lug-rigged fishing boat, related to the ZULU.

NAGASAKI SAMPAN.　　see SAMPAN

NAGGAR　　　　The Naggar is a cargo boat used on the River Nile.

NAO　　　　Nao was the Spanish word for SHIP during the 13th to 16th centuries, not, as some maintain, a term for a specific type of vessel. Contemporary authorities refer to Columbus's ships, in which he crossed the Atlantic in 1492, as Naos, two of which were CARAVELS.

NAPLES TRAWLER.　　see TRAWLER

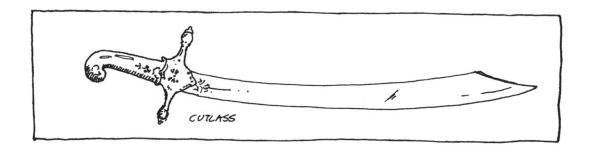

CUTLASS

NAVICELLO (BALANCELLE, BILANCELLA)

A two-masted Italian coasting vessel, the Navicello has an unusual gaff. Instead of being lowered with the mainsail, it is kept standing and the mainsail is hauled out along it on rings.

NEF

A Nef was a French ship of the 15th and 16th centuries developed from and larger than the COG. It was also the word to describe the ship-shaped salt containers made of silver in those days.

NEW ORLEANS LUGGER.   see LUGGER

NICKEY   Nickeys came from the Isle of Man, and were two-masted double-enders used for fishing in the Irish Sea.

MANX NICKEY

NORDLANDS COD BOAT   A Norwegian cod fishing boat, the Nordlands Boat bears obvious affinities to the old VIKING SHIPS.

NORFOLK WHERRY.   see WHERRY

NORTH CHINA JUNK.   see JUNK

NORTH RIVER SLOOP.   see SLOOP

NORWAY YAWL.   see YAWL

NUCLEAR VESSEL   Nuclear-powered vessels are still rare
                      and far from perfection. The
first nuclear-powered merchant vessel was the American
ship **Savannah**, named after the first steamship to cross
the Atlantic.

Savannah

NUGGAR or NUGGER   Nuggars are cargo boats from the
                      lower Nile, similar to GAIASSAS.

THE WHITE STAR STEAMER *Germanic* RECEIVING MAIL IN A GALE
OFF NEW YORK IN THE LATE 1800's   *American engraving*

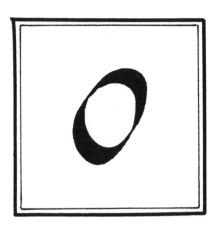

ONE-DESIGN.   see YACHT, RACING

OOMIAK.   see UMIAK

OPIUM CLIPPER.   see CLIPPER

ORA.   see CANOE

OROU.   see CANOE

OUTBOARD MOTORBOAT.   see MOTORBOAT

OUTBOARD RACER.   see MOTORBOAT

A 15TH CENTURY CARRACK   19th century British woodcut

PACIFIC ISLANDS TRADING SCHOONER .   *see SCHOONER*

PACKET BOAT (POST-BARK)   A packet Boat was originally
a boat carrying the mail
regularly between two ports. By the 18th century they were
fast ships. also carrying passengers and going as far as America
and India. They were eventually supplanted by STEAMSHIPS.

AMERICAN PACKET 1830

PADDLE STEAMER

Wheels fitted with some kind of paddle for propelling small boats have been known for thousands of years, so it was to paddles that the first steam engines were connected.

Although a famous Admiralty trial in 1845 between H.M.S. **Rattler** and H.M.S. **Alecto** proved the superiority of the screw over the paddle, paddle steamers remained in use for many years more, especially on rivers and in harbors, where the paddle is actually better since it has more power in reverse than a screw.

Ocean-going paddle steamers were thus gradually eclipsed by screw-propelled vessels, and so probably the best known paddle steamers were the Mississippi River steamers. These were of two types: stern wheelers and side wheelers.

SIDE WHEELER

STERN WHEELER

PADUAKAN   The Paduakan is a KETCH-rigged coasting craft from Celebes.

PAHI   The Tahitians called their large seagoing vessels Pahi. They were usually double CANOES, the sail being supported on two masts, one mast being stepped in each hull.

    The Pahi shown below is an outrigger DUGOUT sailing CANOE from the Society Islands in the Pacific.

PANJANG. *see* SAMPAN

PARANZELLO A Paranzello is an Italian TRAWLER. Usually a two-master, both masts being lateen-rigged, the Paranzello sometimes set a square topsail on the mainmast.

PAREJA The Pareja, like the Italian PARANZELLO above, was also a fishing TRAWLER; used in the Atlantic, the Pareja was common to both Spain and Portugal.

PASSENGER SHIPS (LINER)

In the days of the sailing navies, Liner sometimes meant a SHIP-OF-THE-LINE. Some fishing vessels which worked with lines, rather than nets, were also known as Liners. However, the most common use of the word liner is to describe Passenger Ships which ply a regular route. Before the introduction of steam, PACKET BOATS were sometimes known as Liners. (See also CARGO LINERS.)

In the larger sense, a Passenger Ship is any vessel that carries passengers. This, of course, includes FERRIES, small river-versions of which must have been among the first boats of all. More specifically, Passenger Ship refers to a large, ocean-going vessel whose main purpose is neither naval nor mercantile, but the carrying of paying passengers from one port to another.

In this last sense the Passenger Ship has had the shortest history of many vessels. It is true that PACKET BOATS, which carried passengers as well as the mail, were in regular service by the 16th century, but the pure passenger carrying ship did not appear until well into the latter part of the 18th century.

THE EDDYSTONE LIGHTHOUSE IN THE ENGLISH CHANNEL
ca. 1759

249

The history and development of Passenger ships is largely tied up with that of STEAMSHIPS, for it was with the introduction of steam propulsion that large numbers of people began to travel by sea. Hitherto, sea voyages had been too lengthy and uncomfortable for most people to undertake them for pleasure.

By the beginning of the **19**th century, STEAMSHIPS were making regular voyages across the Atlantic. These early Liners were also fully-rigged sailing vessels. The **Savannah** is usually regarded as the first STEAMSHIP to cross the Atlantic (in **1819**), but she was also a full-rigged ship and in fact seldom used her machinery. It was the **Sirius** who, in **1838**, was the first vessel to cross the Atlantic under steam alone, although she too had sails.

Savannah : 1819

The first large iron ship to be built as a transatlantic liner, screw-propelled, was the **Great Britain** (the first of the very famous Isambard Kingdom Brunel's three shipbuilding masterpieces), launched in **1843**. (The other two were the **Great Western**, **1838**, and the **Great Eastern**, **1858**.)

From this point on, Liners increased in number, size, speed, and luxury, for a little more than a hundred years. The roster of famous Passenger Ships is long and includes many very well-known ships such as the **Oceanic**, **1871**; the **City of Paris**, **1888**; and her sister ship, the **City of New York**; the **Mauretania**, **1906**; and her sister ship, the **Lusitania**; the ill-fated **Titanic**; the **Queen Mary**, **1934**; and her sister ship, the **Queen Elizabeth**, **1938**.

The **United States**, **1951**, was the fastest of the transatlantic liners, with an average speed of over **34** knots. Nowadays, however, most trans-oceanic passengers travel by air, and the days of the great Passenger Ships are over, except for a small number of luxury cruise ships, which are really floating hotels for the rich. Of these ships, perhaps the most well-known is the **Queen Elizabeth II**, or **Q.E.2** as she is more commonly known.

S.S. United States
990' (301 m) 51,821 TONS

PATACHE   The Patache was a coasting vessel from southern Europe, common before the **19**th century. Similar to a **BRIGANTINE**, the mainmast was a single pole, the foremast was in three sections, each carrying a square sail.

PATILE   The Patile is a **BARGE**-like transport vessel used on the Ganges River in India.

PATTAMAR .   see DHOW

PAYANG   The Payang is a native fishing boat from the east coast of Malaysia carrying two black lugsails .

PENJAJAP   The Penjajap is a Malay trading vessel . The two sails are a cross between square sails and dipping lugsails. Bundles of bamboo are carried beneath the bow for stability .

PENTECONTER .   see GALLEY

PERIAGUA .   see PIROGUE

PETER BOAT   The Peter Boat was used on the lower Thames in England for centuries. The hull is a direct descendant of **VIKING SHIPS**, being double-ended, shallow, and beamy.

PILOT BOAT :   Before the advent of steam, a Pilot Boat had to be both fast and seaworthy in order to put the pilot onto an incoming ship first, in any weather. Consequently, early **YACHTS** owe much of their design to these fast sailing boats, which for similar reasons bore much resemblance to the **BALTIMORE CLIPPER**. An American Pilot **SCHOONER** is shown opposite; it should be remembered, however, that other rigs were used, see, for example **PILOT CUTTER** :

Nowadays Pilot Boats vary considerably from country to country, but tend to be small and fast.

AMERICAN PILOT   1885

BRITISH PILOT   1950

~ HAVRE PILOT BOAT

The Pilot Boats used out of Le Havre in France in the days of sail were CUTTER-rigged, fast and very seaworthy.

~ HVALOR PILOT BOAT

Hvalor is in southern Norway; its Pilot Boat was very broad and deep, consequently, a good sea boat. The Hvalor Pilot Boat was spritsail-rigged with a jib and a staysail.

PILOT CUTTER.   see CUTTER

PILOT SCHOONER.   see SCHOONER

PINK   The term Pink applies basically to a small, square-rigged ship with a narrow, overhanging stern, much used for carrying masts.

a.   In the 15th and 16th centuries, Pink was applied to all small ships with narrow sterns.

b.   A little later, the Danish Navy used the word to designate a small **WARSHIP** with a Pink stern, which was, however, broader at deck level in order to accommodate guns.

c.   The term Pink also meant a Dutch herring boat from Scheveningen.

d.   By the 17th and 18th centuries there was a large variety of hulls and rigs which were called Pink, but all sharing the Pink stern.   The Mediterranean Pink, shown below, was a lateen-rigged merchant craft, similar to the XEBEC.

18TH CENTURY PINK

PINKY :   The Pinky, named after the Danish PINK, was one of the oldest New England fishing boats. SCHOONER-rigged, the Pinky had a hull like Baltic boats.

NEW ENGLAND PINKY

~ YARMOUTH PINKY   The Yarmouth Pinky, an English east coast fishing boat is a less extreme example of the Pinky.

PINNACE

a. Pinnace was a class of ship's boat, rowed by eight, and later sixteen, oars, eventually supplanted by the petrol- and diesel-powered small MOTORBOAT.

b. Originating in the 16th century, the pinnace was a small ship of about 20 tons, square-rigged on fore- and main masts, and eventually SCHOONER-rigged. Pinnaces carried oars and were frequently used as ADVICE BOATS.

18 TH CENTURY PINNACE BEING ROWED

PIROGUE or **PIRAGUA (PERIAGUA)** :   Pirogue is the old West Indian name for the DUGOUT CANOE used by the Indians on and around the Gulf of Mexico.

~ LOUISIANA PIROGUE   A direct descendant of the old West Indian Pirogue, the Louisiana Pirogue, made from hollowed-out cypress logs, is used in the swamps and bayous around New Orleans.

~ SENEGAL PIROGUE   The large CANOES used by the natives of Senegal for loading and unloading ships through the heavy surf are known as Pirogues. Manned by as many as **32** paddlers, these giant Pirogues engage in annual races.

~ TAHITIAN PIRAGUA   The Tahitian Pirague,
unlike the other PIROGUES,
is sometimes fitted with an inverted triangular sail.

PLUMB STEMMER.   see SCHOONER, GLOUCESTER FISHING

POCKET BATTLESHIP.   see BATTLESHIP

POJAMA   The Pojama was a swedish WARSHIP from
the 19th century. Similar to a GALLEY,
the Pojama could be rowed, but also had two masts,
and carried two heavy guns in the bow and the stern.
she was similar to the UDEMA.

POLACRE or POLACCA

The Polacre was a ship common to the Mediterranean whose masts were made of single poles, thereby enabling the yards to be raised or lowered to the yards immediately above or below. Most were three-masted, but there were also two-masted versions (BRIGS). In both cases the aftermost mast was lateen-rigged, the other masts being square-rigged.

YARDS

POLACRE WITH ALL SAILS FURLED SHOWING YARDS
CLOSE TOGETHER

POLACRE-SETTEE

A Polacre-settee was a three-masted Polacre, square-rigged only on the mainmast.

PONTOON   Pontoon, which comes from the Latin, meaning *floating bridge*, has acquired a number of specialized nautical meanings:

a.   Pontoon may refer to a flat-bottomed boat used as a LIGHTER or FERRY.

b.   A Pontoon is a specially designed boat to support a temporary bridge.

c.   A Pontoon is a hollow vessel used in raising salvage, by being pumped empty of water and thereby helping to float the salvage.

d.   A Pontoon is a floating structure fixed to the end of piers and jetties to accommodate the rise and fall of the tide.

e.   In the days of sail, a Pontoon was a low, flat vessel fitted with cranes and captans, and used in the cleaning or repair of hulls.

POPO.   see PROA

HAND LEAD

POPOFFKA

The Popoffka, designed by and named for the Russian Vice Admiral Popov, was a circular WARSHIP built in **1875**. The idea was to provide a steady platform for her guns no matter what the state of the sea, but the vessel suffered from a low freeboard and the inability to travel in a straight line when descending rivers, revolving continuously instead.

POST-BARK.   see PACKET BOAT

PRAAM (PRAM or PRAME)

a.   The Pram was a small French coastal GUNBOAT used during the Napoleonic Wars.

b.   Pram is also the word for a very old form of Dutch and Baltic LIGHTER.

___

c. A Pram was a ship's boat of the 16th to 18th centuries.

d. DINGHIES with sawn-off bows, used as TENDERS to YACHTS, are known as Prams.

PRAHU or PRAU (PRAO): Prahu or Prau is a Malayan word meaning boat or vessel, but refers here to those boats found specifically in Malayan waters.

~ FLYING PRAU The Flying Prau was used by Malayan pirates, and could be rowed as well as sailed. The sails were generally made of rattan on bamboo masts.

~ JAVANESE PRAU (PRAO) The Javanese Prau shown on the next page is thought by some to be the possible progenitor of the lateen sail. This vessel is also fitted with outriggers on both sides of the hull.

JAVANESE PRAO

~ MADURA PRAU

near the eastern end of Java,

The Madura Prau, from the island of the same name, is made entirely of teak!

PRAM or PRAME

PRAU BUGIS

The Prau Bugis, from the East Indies, although KETCH-rigged, is a very old type of vessel. The hull is like that of a 'JUNK', and the lower masts are actually tripods.

RUDDERS HUNG
FROM QUARTERS

PRIVATEER

A Privateer was a vessel (and later its crew), which was privately owned and armed, and which, if in possession of a Letter of Marque from the government of its country, was licensed to capture enemy shipping and share in the prize.

The first Letter of Marque was issued in England in **1293**, and because of the effectiveness of privateering on the enemy's merchant shipping, the system continued, until its abolition at the Treaty of Paris in **1856**.

Francis Drake and Paul Jones were only two of many famous seamen who were also Privateers at one time or another.

PRIVATE SHIP   A private ship is a commissioned WARSHIP which, having no flag officer on board, is not a FLAGSHIP.

PRIZE SHIP   A Prize ship is an enemy vessel captured at sea by a WARSHIP or by a PRIVATEER.

PROA :   A Proa is a narrow, double-ended DUGOUT CANOE common to the Micronesian Islands and the Malay Archipelago. Several of the many types are described below. Many Proas have pivoted masts which allow them to be sailed in either direction.

~ BAURUA   The Baurua, now extinct, was a fast Proa from the Gilbert Islands in the western Pacific.

OUTRIGGER

~ FLYING PROA

The Flying Proa came from the Marianas Islands, and was an extremely fast Proa of the reversible mast type.

REVERSED POSITION OF SAIL & MAST

OUTRIGGER

DUGOUT HULL

~ KAEP

The Kaep, from the Palau Archipelago, east of the Philippines, although with a reversible mast, did not have a symetrical hull, one end of which was sailed high out of the water.

269

~ POPO

The Popo is one of the larger and more complicated of the Proas. The hull is flattened on one side and the ends are carved bird heads. Passengers and goods ride on a high, cantilevered platform.

PLATFORM

OUTRIGGER

~ TSUKPIN   Similar to the Kaep in hull form, the Tsukpin has a platform like the Popo. It comes from Yap Island in the Caroline Islands.

~ WA LAP   The Wa Lap, from the Marshall Islands, is also similar to the Popo, and very large, being able to carry as many as fifty people.

PUFFER   A Puffer was a small steam vessel with a very large hold, built on the Clyde in Scotland, and used as a TENDER to the British fleet at Scapa Flow during both World Wars.

PULWAR   The Pulwar is similar to the MALAR PANSHI, and comes from Bengal. Carrying a single large square sail, the Pulwar is steered by an oar.

STEERING OAR

PUNGY.   see SCHOONER

PUNT   There are several different kinds of Punt, but all of them are flat-bottomed with very low freeboard.

a.   The navy Punt was merely a floating platform used for caulking waterline seams of larger vessels.

b.   Punts, with very sharp, pointed bows, are used by wildfowlers in estuaries.

c.   Square-ended punts are poled along and used as pleasure boats.

PURSEINER   (TUNA CLIPPER)

Purseiners are well-equipped, often luxurious, fishing boats which often stay at sea for months at a time fishing for tuna. The largest fleet works out of san Diego, California.

AN ILLUSTRATION FOR SEBASTIAN BRANT'S 'THE SHIP OF FOOLS' 1494
woodcut designed by Albrecht Dürer

Q - BOAT The Q-Boat was a largely unsuccessful experiment of the First World War which was tried again at the outset of the Second World War when it was a total failure. The idea was to fit a small merchant ship with concealed armament and lure to the surface U-BOATS (German SUBMARINES), which would rather attempt to sink the supposed merchant ship by gunfire than by the more difficult process of firing torpedos while still underwater. The U-BOAT having been lured to the surface, the Q-Boat would then open fire and hopefully sink the attacker.

Captain Gordon Campbell won the victoria cross during the First World War for commanding a Q-Boat, but in the Second World War, out of six Q-Boats commissioned, two were sunk, and not a single U-BOAT was even sighted.

QUADRIREME

A Quadrireme was a GALLEY from Greek and Roman times. Although BIREME meant two banks of oars, and TRIREME meant three banks of oars, it is considered unlikely, though not impossible, that quadrireme meant four banks of oars. Rather, it is more likely that the term meant a GALLEY having two men to an oar on two banks.

STERN OF A
GREEK GALLEY

QUINQUEREME

Although no one knows for sure, it is thought most likely that a Quinquereme was a classical GALLEY having three banks of oars (i.e. a TRIREME) with two men on the top oar, one on the middle, and two on the bottom, making five – hence the term Quinquereme. See also PENTECONTER.

QUODDY   The Quoddy was an open keel-boat used for fishing off the Maine coast. The word is an abbreviation of Passamaquoddy Bay, an inlet between New Brunswick and Maine.

AN ILLUSTRATION FOR SEBASTIAN BRANT'S 'THE SHIP OF FOOLS'
1494   woodcut designed by Albrecht Dürer

RACING YACHT. see YACHT

RADEAU   The Radeau was essentially a square-ended scow which could be rigged as a SCHOONER, BRIG, KETCH, or SHIP. Fitted with sweeps and guns, Radeaus were used during the American Revolutionary War as harbor defense vessels.

RADEAU 1776

RAFT   By Raft is usually meant a flat, floating framework or platform. Rafts are used by primitive peoples for transportation; sometimes for loading and unloading ships lying off-shore; and in emergency situations such as shipwrecks.

ABANDONED RAFT

RAM SCHOONER.   see SCHOONER

RANGOON LIGHTER.   see LIGHTER

RASCONA   The Rascona was a two-masted, lug-rigged Venetian cargo boat steered by a steering oar.

RAZEE or RASEE

Razee was the word used to describe a sailing SHIP-OF-THE-LINE WARSHIP which had had her upper works reduced by one deck so that she became a very heavy FRIGATE. This practice was common around the 1830's and 1840's.

RECEIVING SHIP

Receiving ships, which later became known as HULKS, were usually old ships, moored permamently in naval ports, used as barracks for new recruits until they were drafted to seagoing vessels.

REFRIGERATOR SHIP.   see CARGO SHIP

REGISTER SHIP

Spanish ships which traded with the Spanish colonies in America required a licence to do so; the owner's name being entered in a register. Since such ships often carried gold, they were much sought after in time of war by English ships, and were referred to as Register Ships to distinguish them from other Spanish ships.

RESCUE SHIP

Rescue Ships were merchant vessels whose duty was to rescue survivors of torpedoed convoy vessels. They usually traveled in the rear of a convoy and were used during the Second World War.

TYPICAL CONVOY FORMATION

RESEARCH VESSEL.   see FLOATING INSTRUMENT PLATFORM

REVENUE CUTTER.   see CUTTER

RICE BOAT   The Rice Boat of the Irrawadi River in Burma is quite unusual. Since the prevailing wind is a southerly, the boats sail up-river and are punted downstream, the sails being always set for running. The mast is tripod, the square yard curves upwards and is raised by many topping lifts, and the sail is brailed in to the mast!

ROMAN TRADER

Most Roman Traders or merchantmen were of the same basic type : broad, round, with high sterns often carved into swans, and a very forward-leaning foremast from which the artemon sail was set , mainly to assist in steering.

ROUND SHIP

With the exceptions of the fighting ships and the GALLEYS, all medieval ships were known as Round ships ; the average beam being half the length. Round ship was a generic term and included many types such as the COG and the DROMOM.

BEAM

LENGTH

ROWING BOAT : There were a large number of different Rowing Boats used by fishermen and other watermen in the days of sail. They were usually quite different from the small Rowing Boat of today, which is used mainly as a TENDER for YACHTS, and is quite short and light.

Such short and light boats were impracticable when rowing long distances on the open sea since the light boat quickly loses momentum between strokes and the short boat suffers from the constant change in trim as the oarsman changes position.

~ WHITEHALL The Whitehall is probably the most famous of American Rowing Boats. Taking its name from Whitehall street in New York City where the boats were first built, they were for general use in large harbors and bays by all sorts of people, from chandlers and pilots to reporters and agents.

SIDE

STERN · BOW

ROYAL YACHT.   see YACHT

RUA CHALOM   'Rua' is the Siamese word for boat, a Rua Chalom being a small high-stemmed coastal vessel, steered with two oars.

STEM

RUA PET   The Rua Pet, also common to the Gulf of Siam, has a high overhanging bow, and two lugsails.

285

RUA TA

The Rua Ta, like the **RUA CHALOM** and the **RUA PET**, comes from the Gulf of Siam, but is more similar to a **JUNK** than the other two.

SAIC or **SAIQUE**   The Saïc was a small trading KETCH of the 18th to 19th centuries. The mainmast was square-rigged, the mizzen was lateen-rigged.

17 TH CENTURY SAIC

SAILING DINGHY.   see DINGHY

SALVAGE VESSEL   A Salvage Vessel is one engaged in the recovery of ships or cargo that have been lost at sea. Salvage may be accomplished various ways: by making the sunken vessel watertight, and pumping it out until it attains sufficient buoyancy to float itself, or by simply hoisting.

SAMBUK.   see DHOW

SAMOAN CANOES.   see CANOE

SAMPAN :   Some think that the word Sampan comes from two Chinese words, 'san,' meaning thin, and 'pan,' meaning board. Others think it may be of Malay origin. In any event, the sampan is the typical small, light boat of oriental rivers and coastal areas.

Although some of the regional varieties are shown on the following pages, all sampans may be divided into two types: the Harbor Sampan, fitted with a light awning and sculled; and the Coastal Sampan, which has a mast and an often JUNK-like sail. (See BANGKOK SAMPAN, below.)

HARBOR SAMPAN

~ BANGKOK SAMPAN

The Bangkok Sampan is a variety of Coastal Sampan.

~ NAGASAKI SAMPAN

~ SAMPAN PANJANG

Unlike most other sampans, this boat has a keel, and a rudder hung from the stern. It originates from Johore, in Malaysia.

KEEL

~ YANGTZE RIVER SAMPAN

SANDBAGGER

The Sandbagger was a class of RACING YACHT which originated in America around 1850 and became popular in New England waters until the 1880's, although the class persisted in Sydney, Australia until the 1960's. The boat had a large sail plan, and being very shallow, used sandbags as movable ballast to trim the boat on each tack.

BOOMKIN   BOWSPRIT

CAT-RIGGED SANDBAGGER

SARDINE BOAT   Several countries had their own typical Sardine Boats in the days of sail. The Breton lug-rigged boat shown here may be taken as typical although the type varied considerably from place to place and also from time to time. Nowadays, of course, motorized fishing boats are the rule.

SCAPHO   The Scapho was a Greek spritsail-rigged cargo boat with a high, forward-and-aft raking hull.

SCHOKKER
The Schokker began as a Dutch fishing vessel in the early 18th century, and was somewhat similar to the **BOTTER**. It later became popular as a pleasure **YACHT**, and many were built with steel hulls instead of the traditional oak hulls.

SCHOONER :
Although the Schooner began to appear towards the end of the 17th century, the name is said to have originated at the launching of the first vessel of the type at Gloucester, Massachusetts in 1713, when someone is reported to have said : "How she scoons!" or "There she scoons!"

A schooner is a vessel with fore-and-aft sails on properly two masts only, the foremast being shorter than the mainmast, in distinction to vessels like **KETCHES** and **YAWLS** whose foremast is taller (and is actually the mainmast, the aftermast being called the mizzenmast).

MODERN TWO-MASTED SCHOONER

a.   Schooners with jib-headed or jack-yard topsails are known simply as Fore-and-aft Schooners. Though a schooner properly has only two masts, all of the varieties shown below have been made at one time or another.

THREE-MASTED FORE-AND-AFT SCHOONER

FOUR-MASTED FORE-AND-AFT SCHOONER

FIVE-MASTED FORE-AND-AFT SCHOONER

SIX-MASTED FORE-AND-AFT SCHOONER

MAST NAMES:

SPANKER Nº 6   Nº 5   Nº 4   MIZZEN   MAIN   FORE

SEVEN-MASTED FORE-AND-AFT SCHOONER

Thomas W. Lawson
BUILT 1902, LOST 1907

The **Thomas W. Lawson** was the only seven-masted schooner to be built, but was too unwieldy to be successful, and was soon lost.

b.   Schooners were originally rigged with square topsails, and this type is now known as the Topsail Schooner. Advances in rigging design led to jib-headed topsails, as shown on the previous pages, and finally to Bermuda sails which require no topsails at all.

SQUARE TOPSAILS

TOPSAIL SCHOONER (TWO-MASTED)

JIB-HEADED TOPSAILS

GAFF-RIGGED:

BERMUDA-RIGGED:
(NO TOPSAILS)

FORE-AND-AFT SCHOONERS

DEVELOPMENT OF THE SCHOONER

THREE-MASTED TOPSAIL SCHOONER

FOUR-MASTED TOPSAIL SCHOONER

The difference between a four-masted topsail schooner and a four-masted BARQUENTINE is that the BARQUENTINE carries no fore-and-aft sail on the fore mast and the schooner carries no main square sail.

C.   The third main type of schooner rigging is that of the Main Topsail Schooner or Double Topsail Schooner. As the name implies, this is a vessel that carries square topsails on two masts, the term Topsail Schooner being limited to those vessels with square topsails on one mast only. Two examples are shown below.

MAIN TOPSAIL SCHOONER
(TWO TOPSAIL SCHOONER
DOUBLE TOPSAIL SCHOONER)

FIVE-MASTED TWO TOPSAIL SCHOONER

~ BUTTERMAN SCHOONER

The Butterman Schooners carried dairy products from Guernsey to London in the 19th century, and because of fierce competition carried lots of sail and were very fast.

~ CAT SCHOONER

A Cat Schooner carries no headsails (see illustration above), the foremast being set right in the bow. see also CATBOAT.

299

~ CENTERBOARD SCHOONER

The essentials of a schooner rig are two fore-and-aft sails, the aft sail being the bigger, and a headsail (except in the case of the CAT SCHOONER), all other sails being incidental. Now the three main types described at ѣ. have inevitably given rise to numerous varieties, of which the Centerboard Schooner shown below is but one. Aside from having a centerboard, which is a kind of movable keel, the foremast carries not a topsail but a staysail. (See STAYSAIL SCHOONER.)

~ CHESAPEAKE BAY SCHOONER

The Chesapeake Bay Schooner was used in the Chesapeake Bay oyster fisheries.

~ GLOUCESTER FISHING SCHOONER :

Gloucester Fishing Schooners were developed in Gloucester and other Massachusetts Bay ports for market fishing and service on the Grand Banks for cod fishing. Begining around **1846**, a number of distinctive types gradually evolved, which are shown below in chronological rather than alphabetical order.

: ~ FILE-BOTTOM (SHARPSHOOTER)

Modeled after the BALTIMORE CLIPPER, the File-Bottom was so called because of great dead rise (the bottom of the hull being much deeper aft than forward). The first one, the **Romp**, was built by Andrew Story in **1846-7**.

DEAD RISE

RACKING SEIZING

:~ CLIPPER FISHERMAN

As competition increased, speed became essential and a faster Schooner with a larger sail plan was built. This was the Clipper Fisherman, which although fast, capsized easily. Consequently, many lives were lost on this type.

:~ PLUMB STEMMER

In 1884 the safer Plumb Stemmer was introduced with a hull patterned after the PILOT SCHOONERS.

OVERHANGING STERN

(RIGGING AS CLIPPER FISHERMAN)

VERTICAL STEM

:~ **INDIAN HEADER**   Around the late **1890**'s Gloucester
                              Schooners were built with round
stems and a curving keel. The early ones were given Indian
names and the type consequently became known as Indian
Headers.

:~ **KNOCKABOUT**   Eventually the long and dangerous
                           bowsprit was removed, and the last
major type before sail gave way to engine was developed: the
knockabout.

303

~ GREAT LAKES SCHOONER

Two- and three- masted schooners were common on the Great Lakes as cargo carriers throughout the 19th century. Various sail plans were used, but the hulls were usually sharp-ended and of shallow draught. The Great Lakes schooner shown here, carries a raffee sail on the fore-topmast.

RAFFEE

~ JACKASS SCHOONER

Jackass Schooner is the term used for a schooner with no main topmast.

TOP MAST

MAST

FORE TOPMAST

MAIN MAST

FOREMAST

JACKASS SCHOONER WITH NO MAIN TOPMAST

~ PACIFIC ISLANDS TRADING SCHOONER

Pacific Islands Trading Schooners are among the last remaining working Schooners. Usually fitted with auxiliaries and deck houses, they are a varied type, which may be found all over the South Pacific.

~ PILOT SCHOONER

Pilot Schooners were generally fast, shallow-draught vessels with raking masts. Over the period from **1750** to **1900** a number of changes necessarily occured but in general they were very similar to the BALTIMORE CLIPPERS. (see also PILOT BOAT.)

PILOT SCHOONER 1850

~ PUNGY   The Pungy was a local schooner type from the Chesapeake Bay, where it was used for dredging oysters during the last half of the 19th century.

~ RAM SCHOONER (BALD-HEADED SCHOONER)   The term Ram Schooner refers to a schooner whose masts are single poles — there being no topmasts (see illustration under JACKASS SCHOONER).

The term Bald-headed Schooner is sometimes used to mean a Ram Schooner as defined above, although the term bald-headed actually may be used of any vessel under way without her headsails set.

NO HEADSAILS SET

BALD-HEADED SCHOONER
(SECOND DEFINITION)

~ STAYSAIL SCHOONER

The Staysail Schooner is a relatively recent development in which the staysails often carried by large sailing ships are enlarged to the point where they are almost the main sail, the actual mainsail being reduced to a triangular sail no longer attached by its luff to the mast.

STAYSAIL

MAIN FORESAIL

TWO-MASTED STAYSAIL SCHOONER

STAYSAILS

THREE-MASTED STAYSAIL SCHOONER

SCHUYT

The **17**th century Dutch Schuyt was related to the **KETCH**. The **19**th century Schuyt was a small **SLOOP**-rigged sailing boat.

17 TH CENTURY SCHUYT

SCOW

The word scow probably comes from the Dutch, 'Schouw,' which was a shallow-draught, open pleasure boat. Consequently, the word has been used synomomously with **PUNT**, although it also refers to a flat-bottomed **SLOOP**- or **SCHOONER**-rigged American racing **YACHT** used in the **1890**'s.

BIG OVERHANG   BIG OVERHANG

RACING SCOW 1895

SCULLER   The sculler was a small river-boat, which was the 17th and 18th century water taxi in London when the River Thames was used as a main thoroughfare.

SEABOAT   Seaboat is the name used in the Royal Navy to designate ship's boats hung in davits when at sea as opposed to those stowed inboard. They are usually CUTTERS (see CUTTER 5.) or WHALERS, but when used as LIFEBOATS they are so known.

SEALER   A sealer is a vessel designed for the capture and processing of seals. Smaller than WHALE CATCHERS, they are equally strong, having also to cope with Arctic ice.

SELANDER   Together with the DROMON, the selander is one of the vessels that gradually supplanted the TRIREME in the Mediterranean after the fall of the West Roman Empire. The illustration below, although a compilation of crude contemporary sources, is conjectural.

SENEGAL PIROGUE.   see PIROGUE

SEPULCHRAL SHIP   Sepulchral ship is the term used to describe ships used in connection with burial rites. Use of such vessels is worldwide and very ancient. From the ancient Egyptians' and Viking burial ships to the New Zealand Maoris, man has cast his corpses adrift in boats in order that their souls might be carried on to wherever it was believed they would go.

SETTEE   The Settee was a two-masted Mediterranean vessel similar to a GALLEY (and sometimes called a BALANCELLE) used from the 16th to the 19th centuries. The rig was lateen, but the sails were quadrilateral rather than the usual triangular shape — these sails being known as settee sails.

LATEEN SAILS:

TRIANGULAR
LATEEN

QUADRILATERAL
SETTEE

SHALLOP :   Shallop was once a common name applied to various vessels.

a.   The most usual shallop was a small vessel, usually **SCHOONER**-rigged but later more commonly lug-rigged, often used as a **TENDER** to **MEN-OF-WAR** during the time of the sailing navies. The type eventually gave way to the **LONGBOAT**.

b.   The shallop was also a large, heavy undecked boat often made for emergency purposes out of the timbers of a wrecked ship.

c.   The Shallop, or Chaloupe, was a French **GUNBOAT** of the 18th and 19th century. It carried one gun and a crew of about forty.

d.   Small, early American fishing boats were known as shallops.

e.   Shallop was sometimes used to describe a two-man **SKIFF**.

~ FRENCH SHALLOP   The French shallop was a large, decked merchant **SLOOP** - which sometimes carried a small sprit- or lateen-rigged mizzen - used in 18th century Holland and Flanders.

SHARPIE   The sharpie was a very shallow-draught flat-bottomed centerboard boat, originally used in the Connecticut oyster fisheries, and which spread up and down the Eastern seaboard of America. They were variously rigged as CATS, SLOOPS, or SCHOONERS. They were eventually supplanted by power boats.

TWO-MASTED NEW HAVEN
SHARPIE, 1880

SHARPSHOOTER   The Sharpshooter is a small, open workboat from the Bahamas which carries a mainsail and a jib from a long bowsprit.

SHARPSHOOTER.   see SCHOONER, GLOUCESTER FISHING

SHEBEK (CHEKECK)   The shebeck was a late **18** th century Russian adaptation of the Mediterranean **XEBEC**. Whereas most **XEBECS** were completely lateen-rigged, the shebeck was a mixture of lateen-, square, and fore-and-aft rigs. The shebeck could also be rowed and had gun ports.

SHELL   A shell is a very narrow, light rowing craft used for racing. There are one-man shells and shells rowed by eight oarsman and a cox.

SHIP

The word ship comes from the Old English word, 'scip' (pronounced the same as ship), and is the generic term for seagoing vessels as opposed to **BOATS**. The word ship is usually personified as feminine, at least since the 16th century.

The strict nautical definition of ship is more limited, and refers only to a vessel with a bowsprit and at least three masts, all square-rigged.

THREE-MASTED SHIP, 18TH CENTURY

FOUR-MASTED SHIP, 19TH CENTURY

FIVE-MASTED SHIP   preussen : 1902

The **Preussen**, a German ship launched in **1902**, was the only five-masted ship ever built. She carried **47** sails !

SHIPENTINE

A shipentine was a ship (i.e. a vessel with three square-rigged masts) with a fourth fore-and-aft rigged mast. Of course, thought of another way, it could also be called a four-masted **BARQUE**, (i.e. a vessel with at least three masts, the aftermost of which is fore-and-aft rigged, the others being square-rigged).

BARQUE :

⬇

+ EXTRA MAST
= FOUR-MASTED
BARQUE ⇒

SHIP :

⬇

+ EXTRA MAST
=
SHIPENTINE

315

SHIP-OF-THE-LINE.   see WARSHIPS

SHIP-SLOOP

Although both SHIP and SLOOP are distinct types of vessel, the term ship-sloop, which was common in the 19th century, refers to a naval class or rating. In this connection, sloop was the class immediately below that of the FRIGATE class, and thus a ship-sloop was a SHIP-rigged sloop-class vessel, i.e. a smaller SHIP than a SHIP from the FRIGATE class (FRIGATES were also SHIP-rigged).

The apparently confusing term was necessary because sloop-class vessels could also be rigged as BRIGS or SCHOONERS, but never as SLOOPS!

In America the sloop class was called CORVETTE. (see CORVETTE for an illustration of ship-sloop.)

SINGAPORE JUNK.   see JUNK

SINGORA LAKE BOAT

Used on Singora Lake in Malaya, the Singora Lake Boat is a two-masted Siamese type DUGOUT.

PLANK SUPERSTRUCTURE

DUGOUT

SKAFFIE   The skaffie was a Scottish fishing boat. Actually a **LUGGER**, it was similar to the **FIFIE** but flatter-bottomed. It was eventually supplanted by the **ZULU**.

SKIFF

a.   In the British Navy, a skiff was a **SHIP'S** working boat: a small, two-man rowed boat.

b.   Skiff also means a light pleasure boat used on inland waters, usually flat-bottomed.

c.   In America a skiff was a small working boat, fitted with a single spritsail.

NEW JERSEY BEACH SKIFF

SKIPJACK The skipjack, which originated in Chesapeake Bay, was a common East Coast American workboat. The mast was raked aft so that the halyards could be used to hoist cargo on board. **SLOOP**-rigged, skipjacks were superseded by **SHARPIES**.

CENTERBOARD

SKOVSHOVED HERRING BOAT The Skovshoved Herring Boat was a Danish fishing boat with spritsail and topsail and two headsails.

318

SLAVER   vessels used for transporting slaves from Africa to the Americas were known as slavers.   BALTIMORE CLIPPERS were much used, as were other relatively small but fast ocean-going ships.

SLOEP   The sloep was an old Dutch craft of shallow draught used on the canals and in shallow coastal waters.

SLOOP :

a.   During World War II, sloop was a term used to designate a small anti-SUBMARINE convoy ESCORT vessel.*

b.   During the days of the sailing navies, SLOOP referred to the class of vessels immediately below that of FRIGATES. See the articles under SLOOP-OF-WAR, BRIG-SLOOP, SHIP-SLOOP, and CORVETTE.

* This was British usage, in America this kind of vessel was known as CORVETTE.

c.   Sloop is also used to denote a sailing vessel with a
      single mast, fore-and-aft rigged, and carrying a single
headsail, although in America the term also includes vessels
with two headsails, which would be called **CUTTERS** in the rest of
the world. (In America **CUTTER** means the old-fashioned
vessel which carries a jib on a bowsprit.)

6 METER RACING SLOOP

~ BALTIC SLOOP

~ BERMUDA SLOOP

a. From about **1690** until about **1830** the Bermuda Sloop was a very fast boat, especially to windward, much favored by pirates and privateers and used as light CRUISERS by the British Navy in the West Indies.

DOTTED LINE INDICATES
SQUARE SAIL, WHEN SET

b. After **1830** the Bermuda Sloop was a smaller vessel, much used for racing, noted for its excessive sail area

~ FRIENDSHIP SLOOP

Originally an offshore fishing boat built at Friendship, Maine, the Friendship Sloop became popular as a pleasure YACHT, and now there is a Friendship Sloop Association.

~ HUDSON RIVER SLOOP (NORTH RIVER SLOOP)

The Hudson River Sloop, modeled after old Dutch boats, is a shallow-draught, centerboard boat up to **90'(27·5m)** long, used for passengers and cargo on the Hudson before the advent of steam.

Until 1812 these sloops carried square topsails; after that date the triangular topsail proved more convenient. Since these boats were designed for use on the river, the masts are so built and stepped as to allow gybing, a process involving swinging the boom from one side to the other when sailing before the wind, and which invariably dismasts most other vessels. In open waters gybing may be conveniently avoided, but it is often hard to avoid it on a narrow river.

HUDSON RIVER SLOOP

OLD DUTCH CAULKING SPOON

SLOOP-OF-WAR   Sloop-of-war is actually synonomous with the definition given at **b.** under **SLOOP**. Until the 18th century, sloop-of-war meant any small naval vessel that did not fit into any of the other classes. Thereafter, two distinct types evolved, at least in the British Navy, for in America the term remained rather elastic, both types having less than eighteen guns and ranking thus below **FRIGATES**.

The one type was the **SHIP-SLOOP**, rigged as a **SHIP**, with square sails on three masts, and the other type was the **BRIG-SLOOP**, with two masts.

As **TRAINING SHIPS**, sloops-of-war were the last of the navy's sailing ships, lasting until **1904**.

BRITISH BRIG-SLOOP-OF-WAR, 1830

SMACK : The word smack today means any small fishing craft whether driven by sail or engine, but originally it was a fore-and-aft rigged inshore fishing boat, descended from the HOY.

BRITISH FISHING SMACK REEFED DOWN IN A GALE

— LOWESTOFT SMACK The Lowestoft Smack was a KETCH-rigged TRAWLER from the British east coast fishing port of Lowestoft.

SMACKEE

The Smackee is a **SLOOP**-rigged fishing boat common to Key West, Florida.

SNEAK BOX

The Sneak Box was a once-famous boat, used for hunting wildfowl, which sat very low in the water in order to be hidden. The original Sneak Box, also known as a Devil's Coffin, was built at Barnegat Bay in New Jersey, in **1836**.

SNEKKJA.   see ESNECCA

SNOW   The snow, which was a true northern vessel, was
similar to the **BRIG**, which came originally
from the Mediterranean. Usually bigger, the snow carried an
extra mast, the snow mast, immediately abaft the mainmast,
to which was set a gaff-sail. Eventually the two types
combined into the **MAN-OF-WAR BRIG**, which had the square
mainsail of the **BRIG** and the gaff-and-boom mainsail of
the snow.

MAIN MAST
SNOW MAST

SNOW 1770

SÖNDFJORD YAWL.   see YAWL

SÖNDMÖERSK YAWL.   see YAWL

SOUND BOAT

Danish Sound Boats were CUTTER-rigged fishing boats that worked the Kattegat and Oresmund Sound. They were double-enders.

SPERONARA

The Speronara is a lateen-rigged boat with a high vertical stem, from Malta.

SPORT FISHERMAN.   *see* MOTORBOAT

STATE BARGE.   *see* BARGE

STAYSAIL SCHOONER.   *see* SCHOONER

STEAMSHIP   The history and development of the steamship could fill this whole book, but suffice it here to point out that although mechanical means as opposed to wind alone had long been known and tried, it was not until **1807** that the first steamship was put into regular commission. This was the **Clermont**, Robert Fulton's ship, which plied between New York and Albany. Such was the impact of steam, and later other forms of power, that in only a hundred years sail was a thing of the past except for pleasure boats. (But *see* DYNASHIP for a possible return of sail.)

A steamship, then, is a vessel whose motive force is provided by a steam engine. The change from sail to steam was gradual, both being used at first. Eventually steam gave way to more sophisticated forms of power such as in the HYDROFOIL and nuclear-driven vessels.

Clermont: 1807

SUBMARINE :   A submarine is a vessel which can operate beneath the surface of the sea. Designs had existed since the 16th century, but the first working submarine did not appear until 1775. However, it was not until the First World War that submarines were used in any number. (SEE U-BOAT.)

With the advent of nuclear power, the Submarine, though still limited with regard to communications, became totally able to operate and remain underwater indefinitely.

NUCLEAR-POWERED TRITON SUBMARINE
447' (136 m) LONG

~ MIDGET SUBMARINE   Midget or Dwarf Submarines were one- to four-man sub-marines used mainly for harbor attacks.

SUEZ SHORE BOAT

The Suez Shore Boat is a typical Arabian boat from Suez, with a settee sail and a small jib.

SWEDISH FISHING BOAT

The Swedish fishing boat used for mackerel fishing was a double-ended KETCH or YAWL of enormous beam — the beam being three-quarters the length !

A FRENCH CARGO STEAMER OF THE EARLY 1900's   *contemporary engraving*

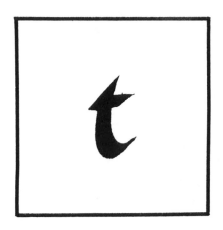

TAHITIAN CANOES.   *See CANOE*

TAHITIAN PIRAGUA.   *See PIROGUE*

TANKER   Although the Chinese carried oil in special JUNKS as long ago as the 18th century, the modern Tanker did not appear until the end of the 19th century. Used for carrying oil, liquified gas, ore, and chemicals, Tankers have grown in size from 5,000 tons in 1912, to 250,000 tons (V.L.C.C., Very Large Crude Carriers) and even 400,000 tons (U.L.C.C., Ultra Large Crude Carriers).

TANKER, 1950

TARTANE

The Tartane is a lateen-rigged Mediterranean coastal trader developed from old Arab cargo boats, which were somewhat larger.

TCHEKTIRME

The Tchektirme is single-masted Turkish coastal vessel

TEA CLIPPER.   see CLIPPER

TENDER   A Tender was a small vessel which serviced a larger ship when in harbor, by carrying cargo, mail, and passengers, to and fro.

Press Tenders were small boats commanded by a lieutenant in the Royal Navy for collecting and delivering impressed men for naval service.

TEPUKEI.   see CANOE

THAMAKAU.   see CANOE

THAMES BARGE.   see BARGE

TOPSAIL BARGE.   see BARGE

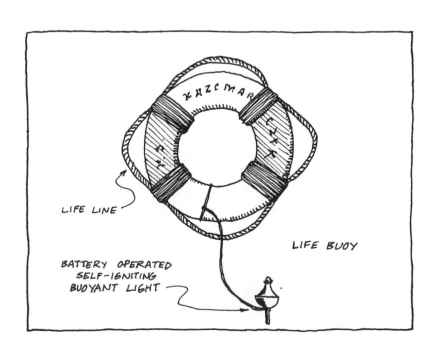

LIFE LINE

LIFE BUOY

BATTERY OPERATED
SELF-IGNITING
BUOYANT LIGHT

TILT BOAT   Before being supplanted by steamers, Tilt Boats were the common English east coast FERRY, carrying passengers between London and such places as Margate and Ramsgate. They got their name from the awning or 'tilt' used to shelter deck passengers.

TILT

TJALK   The Tjalk was a Dutch BARGE-type vessel, similar to the BOEIER, dating from the 17th century.

TJOTTER   The Tjotter is the smallest of the traditional Dutch sailing craft, also much like a very small BOEIER, often used for racing in inland waters.

TONGKANG   The Tongkang is a large, open vessel, used for transporting logs from the East Indies to Singapore. KETCH-rigged, it is a kind of LIGHTER

TONY.   see CANOE

TOPO   The Topo is a flat-bottomed, double-ended small fishing boat once common in Venice. The sail was often brightly colored.

TOPSAIL SCHOONER.   See SCHOONER

TORPEDO BOAT :   Torpedo Boats are naval vessels that attack with torpedos, which are essentially unmanned, underwater, steerable explosives. Robert Whitehead, an English engineer, is credited with having first successfully developed torpedos in **1868.** Immediately thereupon boats were designed to carry and fire torpedos, at first from tubes on the foredeck and then from tubes built into the bows.

TORPEDO TUBE

19TH CENTURY TORPEDO BOAT

~ **MOTOR TORPEDO BOAT (M.T.B., E-BOAT)**   As the various naval powers strove to keep pace with one another, the **TORPEDO BOATS** quickly grew in speed, size, and armament until they turned into **DESTROYERS** by **1900.**

Then in **1904** Britain began building Motor Torpedo Boats, which were once again much smaller craft, to discharge torpedos. However, these boats were at first attached to **CRUISERS** and did not really become effective until, at the end of World War One they were allowed to operate independently.

During the Second World War the Germans developed

338

the Schnellboot, which was called the E-Boat by the British and Americans. Both the M.T.B. (Motor Torpedo Boat) and E-Boat were very fast, being capable of more than **40** knots.

BRITISH MOTOR TORPEDO BOAT 1945

TRABACOLA or TRABACCOLO

The Trabacola was a medium size Adriatic coasting vessel of the **17**th to **19**th centuries. Built in Venice, they carried cargo and occasionally troops.

TRABACOTO   The Trabacoto, popular in the **17**th century, was a small fishing boat from southern Europe, and is thought to have developed from the **GALLEY**. Its settee sails were often brightly colored.

TRAIN FERRY.   see FERRY BOAT

TRAINING SHIP   Training ships may be any sailing ship, from a **BARQUE** to a **BRIG**, maintained by governments for training future sailors.

THE DANISH
TRAINING SHIP
Danmark

340

TRANSPORT SHIP (TROOPSHIP) Transports or Troopships were ships engaged in transporting troops overseas. Originally naval vessels were used, later commercial **LINERS**, and nowadays mainly aircraft.

TRAMP. See CARGO SHIP

TRAWLER : A Trawler is a fishing boat designed to operate a trawl for catching fish which lie near the bottom of the sea.

WARPS

OTTER BOARDS

COD END — NET

A TRAWL

— BRIXHAM TRAWLER

Brixham Trawlers were large KETCH-rigged boats, very good in heavy weather, which worked from Brixham in southern England.

— GIGLIO TRAWLER

The Giglio Trawler was an Italian fishing Trawler, with a typical lateen sail, but a CLIPPER-style bow.

~ HAVRE TRAWLER

The Havre Trawler was a double-ended lug-rigged Trawler used from the French port of Le Havre.

~ LOWESTOFT TRAWLER

Used in the North Sea, the Lowestoft Trawlers have their mainmast stepped further forward than the BRIXHAM TRAWLER.

~ MOTOR TRAWLER

The days of the various sailing Trawlers are gone now, and Motor Trawlers have taken their place. They are now very sophisticated vessels and often travel thousands of miles to their catch.

BRITISH MOTOR TRAWLER

~ NAPLES TRAWLER

used in the Bay of Naples, the Naples Trawler, which is lateen-rigged, set various odd sails in the right weather like other Tuscan and Portuguese craft.

TRIMARAN

A Trimaran is a form of MUTI-HULL, and as such is a development of the CATA-MARAN (d). Trimarans have a central hull and a float on both sides. They are used mainly as ocean YACHTS for racing or cruising. Their lightness and extreme stability make them much faster than similar sized single-hulled boats.

OCEAN-GOING TRIMARAN

TRIREME   The Trireme was a Mediterranean war GALLEY, common from Roman times to the 12th century. There is some confusion as to whether Trireme meant three banks of rowers or three rowers to each oar, the former being the most commonly accepted idea.

TROOPSHIP.   see TRANSPORT

TSUKPIN.   see PROA

TUG   Tugs, originally known as Tug-boats, came into existence after the development of steam power, in the early 19th century.

Although, as the name implies, Tugs pull other vessels, some types, such as the New York Harbor Tugs, are designed to push, and are consequently built with large bow fenders.

There are basically two types of Tugs, illustrated opposite, ocean-going and Harbor Tugs.

OCEAN-GOING TUG

BOW FENDER

FENDERS

HARBOR TUG

TUNA CLIPPER.   see PURSEINER

TUNNY FISHERMAN

In the days before PURSEINERS, Tuna, called Tunny in Europe, was caught from Tunny Fisherman such as the YAWL - rigged French boat from Brittany shown below.

TUINGUTO.   See CANOE

TURRET DECK VESSEL.   See CARGO SHIP

TURUMA

The Turuma was a Swedish vessel, built around 1775, related to the HEMMEMA, the POJAMA, and the UDEMA. They were all combinations of the GALLEY and the MAN-OF-WAR.

The Turuma had twenty-four heavy guns below the oar outriggers and twenty-four swivel guns mounted above the oar outriggers.

SWIVEL GUN

OUTRIGGER

OARS

HEAVY GUNS

UPPER DECK

ROWING DECK

LOWER GUN DECK

GUN ARRANGEMENT
ON TURUMAS

TWAKO or **TWAQO.**   see JUNK

TYNE KEEL.   see KEEL

A FRENCH BATTLESHIP OF THE EARLY 1900'S   a contemporary engraving

U-BOAT   U-Boat was the term used by the allies in the Second World War to designate all enemy SUBMARINES (the allies' vessels being called **SUBMARINES**). The term actually stands for 'Unterseeboot', the German word for SUBMARINE.

A WORLD WAR I GERMAN U-BOAT ON THE SURFACE

UCHE.   see CANOE

UDEMA   The Udema, like the HEMMEMA, the POJAMA, and the TURUMA, was an 18th century Swedish development of the GALLEY. Nine heavy guns were mounted along the center line of the side so that they could be fired to either side over the outriggers for the oars.

UMIAK (OOMIAK)   Umiak is the Eskimo word for CANOE when paddled by a woman. Umiaks are usually larger than KAYAKS, which are paddled by men.

WOOD OR WHALEBONE FRAME

SKIN

UNA BOAT. see CAT BOAT

URCA

a. In the **16**th century an Urca was a Spanish ship, similar to a small **GALLEON**, which was only lightly armed and mainly used to transport stores, chiefly in the Mediterranean.

b. In the **17**th and **18**th centuries an Urca was a flat-bottomed, very high-sterned boat of about **300** tons, carrying six or so guns. These Urcas, which would have been called **FLY-BOATS** by the Dutch, were used chiefly as **DISPATCH BOATS.**

KNIGHTHEAD 1691

A CLIPPER SHIP

early 20th century French engraving

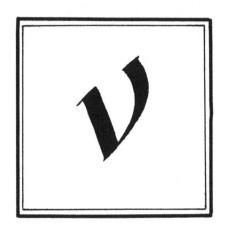

VAKA.   see CANOE

VANAGI.   see CANOE

VELOCERA   The Velocera is an Italian coasting vessel
distinguished by sometimes being rigged with
all three major rigs: square, fore-and-aft, and lateen.

VESSEL   A vessel is a **CRAFT** or **SHIP** of any kind, but usually larger than a **ROWING BOAT** and often restricted in meaning to something which plies larger rivers and lakes and the sea.

VICTORY SHIP.   see CARGO SHIP

VICTUALLER   In the days before much was known of food preservation, Victuallers, which were usually merchant ships taken up for the purpose, were required to accompany or supply ships in time of war or on long cruises.

In the case of long voyages, the Victuallers would often be broken up when they had delivered their stores, as was the case at the Straits of Magellan on Drake's first voyage around the world in 1577.

VIKING SHIP :   There are rock carvings of Scandinavian boats which date from 2000 B.C. and which show features similar to later Viking ships, e.g. curved ends and carved animal heads.

By the time of the vikings (600 - 1,000 A.D.) there were several distinct types, examples of which have been preserved, such as the **Oseberg Ship**, the **Gokstad Ship,** and the **Nydam** and **Kvalsund Boats**, all of which are now in museums.

Karvs and **Knorrs** were **MERCHANTMEN** and coastal trading vessels, which ranged in size from ten- or fifteen-oared boats up to thirty-oared boats, which could carry crews of two hundred.

A typical **8**th century Viking **MERCHANTMAN** is shown opposite.

~LONGSHIP   The Longship or Drekki (see **DRAGON**)
was the Norse or Viking **GALLEY** used
for raiding and war purposes. These ships pulled up to eighty
oars and traveled as far as Greenland and North America.

357

VINCO

The Vinco was a three-masted POLACRE-rigged ship from Genoa, Italy, common in the 19th century.

WA .　　　see CANOE

WA'A .　　　see CANOE

WAGA .　　　see CANOE

WAKA .　　　see CANOE

WAKA TAUA .　　　see CANOE, MAORI WAR

WA LAP.　　　see PROA

WARSHIPS (MAN-OF-WAR , SHIP-OF-THE-LINE) : The term Warship

in its most general sense means any ship or vessel either designed for or employed in war.

Until approximately **1000** B.C. , it would appear from such evidence as is available that EGYPTIAN CRAFT (the earliest ships of which we have any record) were single-design vessels , the same vessel being used for war, commerce, or pleasure.

EGYPTIAN SHIP CIRCA 1500 B.C.

For the next two or three thousand years Warships were chiefly GALLEYS. It was the Phoenicians who developed the war GALLEY, presumably from earlier EGYPTIAN CRAFT.

The war GALLEY was rowed by banks of rowers, and had as its main weapon a pointed ram at or just below the water level which was used to sink enemy vessels. Fighting was done by archers and stone slingers.

War GALLEYS increased in size under the Carthaginians, the Greeks, and the Romans; and various types, such as BIREMES,

TRIREMES, and QUADRIREMES, etc. were developed.

PHOENICIAN WAR GALLEY   400 B.C.

GALLEYS as warships lasted well into the 18th century in the Mediterranean but had virtually disappeared in northern seas by 1000 A.D., the last practical examples (except for a few odd hybrids such as the POJAMA and the CONTINENTAL GALLEY) being the VIKING LONGSHIPS. These ships, being also sailed, were not strictly GALLEYS, although the oar was the main means of propulsion. VIKING LONGSHIPS had no ram.

VIKING LONGSHIP   1000 A.D.

While GALLEYS, and their relations, GALLEASSES, reigned supreme as warships in the Mediterranean, the sailing warship of the north was relatively slow to develop. At first, when ships were needed for war, the practice was to hire regular merchant ships for the occasion.

The introduction of gunpowder provided the warship with its own weapon, and made the ship more than a means of transportation. Consequently, ships were built specifically to carry guns.

At first, these early warships had low freeboard, and guns mounted on platforms in the bow and stern. But as the guns increased in size and number it was found necessary, for stability, to mount the guns amidships.

This led to the building of ships with high castles in the bow and stern to provide a better field of fire for small guns and muskets, and also to provide protection against boarders attempting to enter the ship by the low waist.

13TH CENTURY ENGLISH WARSHIP WITH CASTLES

1520 PORTUGUESE MAN-OF-WAR Santa Catarina do Monte Sinai
REPRESENTING THE PEAK OF DEVELOPMENT OF 'HIGH-CHARGED
SHIPS'

363

The two preceding illustrations show how far the idea of building castles in the bow and stem was carried. By the early 16th century cannon were mounted on board and gunports were cut in the sides so that cannon could be mounted on a gun deck below the upper deck.

At this point in history ships began to be fought by their own crews instead of merely carrying soldiers to fight, although musketeers still fought from the 'castles'.

Such ships as the famous English warship **Henry Grâce à Dieu**, launched in **1514**, and the Portuguese warship **Santa Catarina do Monte Sinai**, shown on the previous page, could now be called Men-of-War, and were known as HIGH-CHARGED SHIPS.

The next major development was the introduction of LOW-CHARGED SHIPS, designed by Sir John Hawkins in **1585**. LOW-CHARGED SHIPS did away with the high forecastles and were consequently faster and better able to sail close to the wind.

Other maritime nations quickly followed England's lead and the basic warship design remained virtually unchanged for the next three hundred years, increasing only in size.

HIGH-CHARGED SHIP
PRE - 1585

LOW-CHARGED SHIP
POST - 1585

After Sir John Hawkins' innovative design in **1585**, there was little change in warships except for a gradual increase in size and sail area.

By the mid-**18th** century most European nations classified their warships into six rates according to the number of guns they carried.

Lord Anson, during his first term* as First Lord of the Admiralty, introduced the following rates: (The figures in brackets reflect the changes made in **1810**.)

FIRST RATE :	100 (110) GUNS OR MORE
SECOND RATE :	84 (90) TO 100 (110) GUNS
THIRD RATE :	70 (80) TO 84 (90) GUNS
FOURTH RATE :	50 (60) TO 70 (80) GUNS
FIFTH RATE :	32 TO 50 (60) GUNS
SIXTH RATE :	ANY NUMBER OF GUNS UP TO 32

Ships of the first three rates were considered powerful enough to lie in the line of battle when fleets engaged battle, and were thus known as ships-of-the-Line.

Fourth rate ships were rare, and only occasionally used as ships-of-the-Line.

Fifth and sixth rate ships were known as **FRIGATES**; but sixth rate ships, if only commanded by a Commander, and not a Captain, were known as **SLOOPS**. All rates were three-masted.

* **1751-6**

MAN-OF-WAR
18TH CENT. 1ST RATE (100 GUN)
SHIP-OF-THE-LINE

ADMIRAL LORD NELSON

The invention of the first efficient steam engine by James Watt in **1769** led gradually to the abandonment of sails. At first steam was little used by warships since paddle-wheels were too vulnerable. But with the introduction of the propeller, the superiority of which was proved in a famous tug-of-war in **1845** between the two Royal Navy steam SLOOPS, **H.M.S. Rattler** (propeller-driven) and **H.M.S. Alecto** (paddle-driven), most warships had steam engines installed.

At first steam was considered auxiliary to sail; and then for a long time sail was retained as auxiliary to steam.

From the middle of the **19**th century, (after the destruction of a wooden Turkish fleet by Russian shells at the Battle of Sinope in **1853**) warships were built with at first iron and then steel hulls.

Sails finally disappeared just before the end of the century.

H.M.S. Inflexible : 1887

Once Warships were being made of steel and driven by engines, their armament also increased. The muzzle-loaded naval cannon, mounted on a wooden carriage, gave way to long-range breech-loading guns firing explosive shells instead of solid shot.

The Man-of-War had been supplanted by the BATTLESHIP. In fact, after 1900, most navies now classed their Warships into BATTLESHIPS, AIRCRAFT CARRIERS, CRUISERS, DESTROYERS, and FRIGATES. The old order of Ships-of-the-Line was gone.

EARLY 20TH CENTURY WARSHIP
FRENCH BATTLESHIP
Jauréguiberry

After 1900, warship development grew ever faster. Steam engines gave way to high-speed turbines and guns increased in size and range. However, an entirely new form of warship was about to appear; the SUBMARINE.

By the end of the First World War the SUBMARINE was well on its way to becoming the dominant naval weapon of the 20th century, although it sounds a little odd to call it a warship.

GERMAN SUBMARINE 1914-18

A few years after the introduction of the SUBMARINE, aircraft began operations from ships and AIRCRAFT CARRIERS came into being. These developed into the biggest warships ever built.

However, the increased use of long-range guided missiles brought an end to huge ships. Especially as missiles were developed which could be fired from SUBMARINES, so a reduction in the size of warships ensued.

It seems likely that the function of the old warship will in the future be divided between underwater striking units and small, versatile, nuclear-powered surface ships.

369

MAINMAST

QUARTER DECK

UPPER DECK

MIDDLE DECK

LOWER DECK

ORLOP

HOLD

SECTION AMIDSHIPS (LOOKING FORWARD) OF AN
ENGLISH FIRST RATE SHIP-OF-THE-LINE, 18TH CENT.

WEATHER SHIP Weather ships were originally obsolescent WARSHIPS such as SLOOPS, FRIGATES, and CUTTERS, which stayed in one place at sea to measure things like barometric pressure, temperature, and wind velocity. Later, special vessels were built for these purposes although today much meteorological information is gathered by satellite.

WEST INDIAMAN West Indiaman was the name given to any ship regularly plying the trade route between Europe and the Caribbean (West Indies). Compare EAST INDIAMAN.

WEST RIVER CHINESE JUNK. See JUNK

WHALEBOAT In the days when whales were hunted from sailing ships, these ships were known as WHALERS. Every WHALER carried a number of open, double-ended whaleboats from which the actual harpooning was done.

Later the term was applied to similarly built open boats used for coastal work; the fact that they were double-ended making it possible to beach them bow-to or stern-to.

WHALEBOAT 1800-1850

WHALE CATCHER

Nowadays, whales are hunted from whale Catchers, which act as TENDERS to a large WHALE-OIL FACTORY VESSEL. The whale Catchers are used entirely for harpooning the whales, which are then brought to the factory ship for processing.

HARPOON

WHALE-OIL FACTORY VESSEL

A whale-oil Factory Vessel is a large modern vessel for processing whales as they are caught by the attendant WHALE CATCHERS.

NORWEGIAN WHALE FACTORY SHIP
638.5' (194.5 m) LONG

372

WHALER or WHALING SHIP

Whaler was the generic name given to ships of all types engaged in the whaling industry. The old whaler caught whales with the help of small WHALEBOATS. The modern whaler (WHALE-OIL FACTORY VESSEL) uses WHALE CATCHERS to catch the whales. While all these vessels may be called whalers, there is no distinct type known as a whaler.

Today, however, there are two broad meanings to the term whaler which are more specific. The first refers to the old sailing ships of many types, which hunted whales. The second refers to a WARSHIP'S boat.

TANCOCK WHALER (SCHOONER)

WHALEBOATS

AMERICAN WHALING SHIP
1840 (SHIP)

373

WHERRY: The wherry was at first a light, open ROWING BOAT, used on the lower reaches of the River Thames in the 17th and 18th centuries. Somewhat resembling the Turkish CAIQUES, the Wherry was a gentleman's boat, and as such was soon introduced to the colonies.

ADMIRALTY WHERRY, 1697
10'6' (3.2 m) LONG

~ NORFOLK WHERRY The Norfolk Wherry is a large, shallow-draught, freight-carrying BARGE used on the Norfolk Broads in England (compare the THAMES BARGE).

WHITEHALL. *see ROWING BOAT*

WINDJAMMER *Windjammer is a non-nautical name by which square-rigged sailing ships are sometimes known.*

WINDSURFER *The windsurfer is a kind of sailing surfboard, sailed by balancing upright on the board and holding on to the boom.*

WOOL CLIPPER. *see CLIPPER*

WRECK VESSEL *A wreck vessel is a moored vessel, usually with no means of self-propulsion, situated over a wreck which would otherwise be a danger to navigation.*

UNLOADING BANANAS IN 19TH CENTURY NEW YORK   American engraving

X-CRAFT.   see SUBMARINE, MIDGET

XEBEC   The xebec was a Mediterranean sailing descendant of the GALLEY, much used by corsairs from the 16th to the 19th centuries. Their rig varied from square to lateen, according to the wind, which necessitated much work and large crews – up to three and four hundred men for a twenty-four-gun boat.

SPANISH XEBEC 1760

A 19TH CENTURY STEAMER DELIVERING PAPERS TO THE FIVE FATHOM LIGHTSHIP   American engraving

YACHTS : The word Yacht comes from the Dutch word, 'jachten' meaning to hunt, to hurry. (The 17th century Dutch JACHT was used as a fast DISPATCH BOAT.)

When Charles II was restored to the English throne in **1660** the city of Amsterdam (where he had been staying during the time of the British Commonwealth) presented him with the Yacht **Mary**. This Yacht, which had originally been built for the East India Company, was a private pleasure boat, related to the **ESNECCAS**, vessels used to "convey" princes, ambassadors or other great personages from one kingdom to another" (Falconer's Marine Dictionary, 1771).

So from 1660 on, the word Yacht was used to denote a small, fast, pleasure boat.

~ CRUISING YACHT

Cruising Yachts are built in many sizes and varying rigs, from small two-berth boats to vessels, capable of world circumnavigation, which are very well equipped with all kinds of electronic navigational aids and auxiliary engines.

ENGLISH CRUISING SLOOP YACHT
21' (6.4m) LONG

~ DAY SAILER

A Day Sailer is the name given to pleasure Yachts designed solely for pleasure sailing of short duration. There are no cabins and no accommodations, although sometimes part of the boat forward is decked over to provide a small shelter and sometimes to enclose a head.

Day sailers, like the one opposite, are usually no larger than **21' (7m)**.

SLOOP DAY SAILER
16'9" (5.11m)

~ICE YACHT

Ice Yachts actually ride on skates on frozen bodies of water such as lakes.

~ MOTOR YACHT

Motor Yachts do not have sails and are usually very luxurious personal cruising vessels such as the **Vedette**, shown below, which was built for Fred W. Vanderbilt in **1924**. Royal YACHTS are today usually Motor Yachts.

MOTOR YACHT *Vedette*: 1924

~ RACING YACHT :

There are probably as many different Racing Yachts as there are vessels described in this book. The following entries are therefore merely a sampling of some of the better-known kinds.

It is human nature that so often compells two of almost anything that moves to race, and consequently it is fairly safe to say that probably every kind of craft has been raced; the Racing Yacht is distinguished only by having been designed solely towards that end, often sacrificing qualities normally requisite such as comfort, room, and even seaworthiness.

: ~ AMERICA'S CUP YACHT

Probably the best-known Racing Yachts are those that compete for the America's cup.

The America's Cup is a trophy originally presented by the Royal Yacht Squadron in **1851** for a race around the Isle of Wight. The American SCHOONER **America** won the cup and the cup has never been won back from the New York Yacht Club, although more than twenty challenges have been made.

Competitors were at first yachts of the largest class, but since the Second World War the yachts concerned have all been of the International 12-meter Class (**39'**)

SCHOONER YACHT America: 1851

12-METER SLOOP YACHT Constellation
(1964 WINNER)

383

:~ INTERNATIONAL DRAGON CLASS

International Dragon Class Yachts are ONE-DESIGN YACHTS designed by Johan Anker in **1928**. They were widely popular until the recent introduction of less-expensive Yachts.

INTERNATIONAL DRAGON CLASS YACHT, 1965
29.2' (8.88 m) LONG

:~ INTERNATIONAL METER CLASS

International Meter Class Yachts are designed to rate as **12, 10, 8, 6,** or **5.5** meters according to the International Yacht Racing Union rules.

The rating is not a measure of length so much as the result of a formula, which includes the yacht's overall length, the waterline length, breadths at different points, depths inside the hull, draught, total displacement, and sail height and area.

:~ J-CLASS YACHT

J-Class Yachts were the largest yachts built under the **1925** international rating rule. They represented the peak of yacht racing but only lasted a short while due to the huge expense involved.

J-CLASS YACHT Ranger 16TH AMERICA'S CUP WINNER, 1937 (135' (41.1m))

:~ ONE-DESIGN

A One-Design Class Yacht is a member of a class in which all the other boats are as nearly identical as possible. The purpose is to make the race resultant upon the individual skills of the helmsman and crews.

There are hundreds of different one-Design classes from tiny **12' (3.6m)** Sailfish to the big one-tonners.

~ ROYAL YACHT

Royal Yachts are vessels provided for the use of royalty and have been used for a very long time. Their origins go back to the ESNECCAS of the 12th century.

Since the advent of steam, Royal Yachts are propelled by engines and are not sailing vessels. The British monarchy, like those of other nations, has had many Royal Yachts, the present one being H.M.Y. *Britannia*, launched in 1953.

THE BRITISH ROYAL YACHT *Britannia*

YANGTZE RIVER SAMPAN. see SAMPAN

YARMOUTH PINKY. see PINKY

YARMOUTH YAWL. see YAWL

YAWL : The word Yawl appears to come from the Middle Low German, 'jolle,' or the Dutch, 'jol,' and meant either a small ship's boat, like a PINNACE, or just a small sailing boat.

Apart from the particular Yawls mentioned below, the word today refers to any two-masted boat having a main-mast, and a small mizzen mast abaft the steering gear (in distinction to a KETCH, whose mizzen mast is stepped forward of the steering gear. This Yawl rig is popular on pleasure YACHTS.

CENTER COCKPIT
& STEERING GEAR

MIZZEN

MAIN

YAWL-RIGGED CRUISING YACHT

~ NORWAY YAWL (ARENDAL YAWL)   The Norway Yawl is an open SKIFF used as a small fishing boat around Arendal, Norway.

~ SÖNDFJORD YAWL

The Söndfjord Yawl is an open, double-ended, Norwegian herring fishing boat.

~ SÖNDMÖERSK YAWL

The Söndmöersk Yawl was similar to the old VIKING SHIPS. It was double-ended, with high, ornamental stem and stern posts. It was an open fishing boat from the west coast of Norway.

~ YARMOUTH YAWL   The Yarmouth Yawl is descended from the Scandinavian Yawl, but is much bigger. Used off the coast of Norfolk in England, these three-masted, double-enders could make **16** knots.

YARMOUTH YAWL, 1850

YAWL BOAT   The Yawl Boat was carried in davits from the stern of coasting vessels. It was an open, rowed boat, later supplanted in fishing vessels by the DORY.

YORKSHIRE LUGGER.   see LUGGER

THE EAST RIVER, NEW YORK

19TH century engraving

ZARUG or **ZARUK.**   see DHOW

ZULU   The Zulu was a compromise between the FIFIE and the SKAFFIE, which were also lug-rigged Scottish fishing boats. The Zulu was introduced by a boatbuilder called Cameron during the Zulu War (1878-1879), hence the name.

BILANDER AND KETCH   *from* ELEMENTS AND PRACTICE OF RIGGING
AND SEAMANSHIP *by* STEEL, 1794

Readers' Additions

While every encyclopedia aims at completeness, no one author can know everything and it is inevitable that omissions will occur. This space is to note any such omissions, which, if brought to my attention, I will endeavor to include in any future editions of this work.

Glossary

NOTE: This is a glossary of only those sails and nautical terms found in the A to Z section of this book. It is by no means an exhaustive nautical dictionary, for which the reader is referred to the Bibliography following this section.

ABAFT	towards the stern, relative to some other object or position.
AFT	towards or at the stern, in a general rather than relative sense.
AFTERMAST	that mast, in a two- or more masted vessel, which is nearest the stern.
AFTERMOST	most aft.

AMIDSHIPS   in the middle of the ship, whether longitud- inally or laterally.

ANCHOR   a large and heavy object, attached to the ship by a cable, designed to hold the ship in one place by digging itself into the sea bed.

ANCHOR DECK   a special deck built in the bows of a ship to hold the anchor and its cable.

ARTEMON   a small square sail set on a yard and carried below a sharply steeved spar over the bows of a Roman merchantman.

YARD
SHARPLY STEEVED SPAR
BOWS
ARTEMON

ROMAN MERCHANTMAN: A.D. 50

ASTROLABE   an instrument used to take the altitude of the sun and the stars in medieval navigation, illustrated on page 23.

BALANCE LUGSAIL a lugsail, the tack of which is at the mast and the foot of which is laced to a boom, in contrast to a dipping lugsail which has no boom and the tack of which extends forward of the mast.

BALANCE LUGSAIL

BALLAST additional weight carried in a vessel to increase stability and to provide a satisfactory trim fore and aft.

BATTEN a. thin iron bars used to secure the hatch covers.
b. thin wooden or plastic strips which fit into pockets in the leech of a Bermuda mainsail to hold it out.

BATTEN DOWN, TO   the process of securing the openings in the deck and sides of a vessel when heavy weather is forecast.

BEAK   the name given to the metal point or ram fixed on the bows of warships used to sink other ships.

BEAKHEAD   the space, in a sailing warship, immediately forward of the forecastle. This space, in the very front of the ship was open to the sea and was used as the seaman's lavatory, hence the term, still in use, of "head" for all lavatories on board.

BEAM   the transverse measurement of the widest part of a vessel.

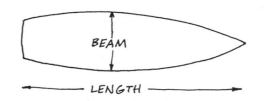

BERMUDA SAIL   a very tall triangular sail common originally on sailing craft around Bermuda.

BLOCKADE in maritime warfare blockade means the interception of enemy trade. Before the invention of the long-range gun it was virtually synonymous with "investment," which was the patrolling of an enemy port to prevent movement in or out.

BOARD, TO to go on board, to go into a ship.

BOOM a. a spar to which the foot of the mainsail, the foresail, or mizzen is set

MAINSAIL   FORESAIL
FOOT OF SAIL
BOOM

b. the spars which connect outriggers to the main hull are called booms.

HULL
BOOM
OUTRIGGER

DUGOUT CANOE WITH OUTRIGGER

c. also the name of a barrier floating at water level across a harbor entrance to block it.

BOOMKIN   a short spar extending horizontally from the stern, . to which overhanging sails may be attached.

BOW   the foremost end of a vessel, often used in the plural. The end opposite the stern.

BOW DOORS   doors in the bow of a ship through which men and armaments may be loaded and unloaded. See illustrations on pages 201 and 202.

BOW FENDER   something let down between the bows and another ship or wharf to prevent chafing. See illustration on page 347.

BOWSPRIT   (pronounced bohsprit), a large spar extending forward over the bows of a ship to provide the means of staying (making secure) the foremast, and from which the jibs are set.

BOW-TO   with the bows leading.

BRAIL, TO   to haul in the brails - ropes leading around the sail to the mast - so that the sail may be temporarily furled against the mast.

BRIDGE   in the days of sail a ship was controlled from the steering wheel located in the stern, but when steam propulsion was introduced it was found that a better view was obtained from the bridge which connected the side paddle wheels. When the propeller replaced paddle wheels the bridge structure was retained as the best place from which to control the ship.

CABIN   a room or space in a ship, partitioned off to provide a private apartment for sleeping or eating.

CAISSON   a floating platform or tank which can be submerged and floated again. Caissons have several applications, such as floating submerged objects, providing a means of working on underwater structures, and closing the entrance to a dry dock.

CANOE STERN   having a stern shaped like a canoe.

CAPSTAN   a cylindrical barrel fitted on deck in larger ships for heavy lifting work, such as raising the anchor.

CAPSTAN BARS — DRUMHEAD — CAPSTAN — WHELPS

CARRONADE   a short, light carriage gun used by the Royal Navy during the late 18th and early 19th centuries.

CARVEL-BUILT   a wooden vessel in which the side planks are all flush, as compared with clinker-built, in which the side planks overlap.

CENTERBOARD   a device which is lowered in a boat of shallow draught to increase its lateral area and its resistance to leeway, or sideways motion.

CENTER-OF-EFFORT   a point on the sail through which the maximum wind force acts.

CLINKER-BUILT   a method of boat construction in which the side planks overlap.

COME ABOUT, TO   the operation of pointing a sailing vessel ever closer into the wind until finally the bows swing round and the wind is taken over the other side.

CON, TO   the action of looking out and navigating, as in the conning tower of a submarine.

CONVOY   one or more merchant ships sailing in company under the protection of naval ships.

DAVIT   a small crane, at the side of a vessel, used to carry, lower, and raise small boats such as lifeboats.

DECK   the flooring of a vessel.

DECKHOUSE   an enclosed structure or cabin built not within the hull but on the top deck of a vessel.

DIPPING LUG FORESAIL   a dipping lugsail used as the sail on the foremast of a two- or more masted vessel.

DIPPING LUGSAIL   a lugsail, the tack of which extends forward of the mast, necessitating the dipping (lowering) of the sail when coming about so that the sail may be set on the other side of the mast.

DIPPING LUGSAIL

DOUBLE-ENDED   with the stern similar to the bow, as with a canoe.

DOUBLE-OUTRIGGER   a vessel, such as a native canoe of the Pacific and Indian Oceans, having a counterpoising log rigged out from both sides to provide stability.

DRAUGHT   (sometimes written 'draft' in American), the depth of water which a ship draws.

FIGUREHEAD   an ornamental carved figure erected on the bows of a vessel, generally expressing some aspect of the ship's name or function. An old superstition that a naked woman could calm an angry sea led to many figureheads of women with bared breasts.

FIVE-MASTED, FIVE-MASTER   a sailing vessel having five masts from which sails are set.

FLAG OFFICER   any officer in any navy of the rank of rear admiral (or the equivalent) and above; such officers, when in command at sea, denote their presence by flying a flag, in distinction to commodores, who fly broad pendants.

FLAGSHIP   the ship, in navies, that carries the admiral's flag. In mercantile shipping lines, the senior captain's ship.

FLEET   a group of vessels sailing together. The word is also sometimes used to describe all the vessels of a navy, e.g. the Russian fleet, or all the vessels of a similar type, e.g. the German U-boat fleet.

FLIGHT DECK   the deck, on an aircraft carrier, from which the planes take off and land.

FLUSH-DECKED   a vessel, the top deck of which runs unbroken from stem to stern, with bridge or wheelhouse amidships.

19 TH CENTURY FLUSH-DECKED CARGO SHIP

FOOT   the bottom edge of a triangular or four-sided sail.

FORE-AND-AFT   in the same direction as a line running from the bows to the stern, i.e. lengthwise.

FORE-AND-AFT MAINSAIL   a mainsail which lies in a fore-and-aft direction, as in a modern yacht, in distinction to a square sail which lies across the vessel.

FORE-AND-AFT RIGGED   a vessel in which the sails are arranged so that the luffs of the sails abut the masts or the stays.

FORE-AND-AFT SAIL a sail set with the luff or leading edge to the mast or stay, as opposed to a square sail which is hung from a yard set at right angles to the mast.

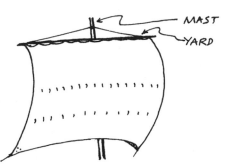

FORE-AND-AFT SAIL   SQUARE SAIL

FORECASTLE (pronounced fohcsal), the space below the deck in the bows of a ship. The word originated from the 'castle' which was built in the bows of medieval fighting ships, and from which the archers fought.

FORECASTLE DECK (pronounced fohcsal deck), the short deck above the forecastle in the bows of a ship.

FOREDECK in a ship with no raised forecastle deck, the foremost part of the deck is known as the foredeck.

FOREFOOT   the point at which the stem joins the forward
end of the keel.

FOREMAST   the first mast aft the bow, although
if the second mast is smaller it is
called the mizzenmast and the first mast, though still
technically the foremast, is called the main mast.

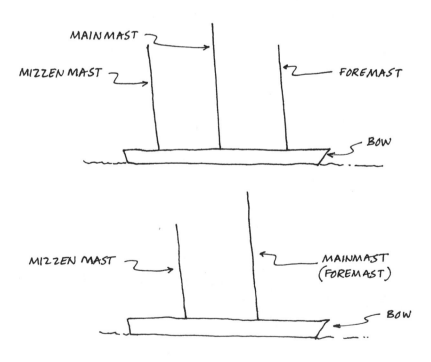

FORE-TOPMAST   the uppermost part of the foremast.

FORWARD   (pronounced forrard), towards the bows of a ship, or in the fore part of a ship.

FOUR-MASTED, FOUR-MASTER   a sailing vessel having four masts from which sails are set.

FREEBOARD   the distance from the top of the uppermost deck to the waterline, properly measured at the waist or center of the ship.

FULL-RIGGED   properly a full-rigged ship has at least three masts, each fitted with a topmast, topgallant mast, and royal mast, all square-rigged with yards and square sails.

GAFF   a spar to which the head of a four-sided fore-and-aft sail is set, and hoisted by.

GAFF
HEAD OF SAIL
BOOM

GAFF AND BOOM MAINSAIL   a four-sided fore-and-aft mainsail which has a gaff and a boom, as illustrated above.

GAFF MAINSAIL   a four-sided fore-and-aft mainsail, having a gaff (but not necessarily a boom).

GAFF-RIGGED   a vessel rigged with four-sided, fore-and-aft sails laced to gaffs.

GAFF SAIL   a four-sided fore-and-aft sail which is laced to a gaff.

GUN DECK   a deck on which guns are mounted. Ships may have but one or several gun decks, see illustration on page 370.

GUNWALE   (pronounced gunnel), strictly, the gunwale is the plank which covers the heads of the side timbers of a ship, but its meaning has been extended to mean the extension above the deck of the sides of a small vessel.

HALF-DECK   originally the structure on the upper deck of a merchant vessel where apprentices were berthed, the term now refers to any deck which extends over only part of the ship.

HALYARDS   (also spelt halliards or haulyards), ropes, wires, or lines used to hoist or lower sails.

HARD-CHINE   a hull having a pronounced angle at the point where the sides meet the bottom.

CROSS-SECTION OF HARD-CHINE HULL

HARPOON   a spear with a barbed head and a line attached used for catching whales.

HATCH   although often used to mean the cover that closes it, a hatch is properly an opening in the ship's deck designed for ingress and egress of people or cargo.

HEAD   a.   the top edge of a four-sided sail.

b.   originally used in the plural to refer to the space forward of the forecastle used as the seaman's lavatory, the word is still used in this sense though lavatories are no longer open or neccessarily located in the same place.

HEADSAIL   a sail hoisted at the forward end of a vessel such as a jib or staysail.

HEEL   the point at which the keel meets the sternpost.

STERNPOST

HEEL   KEEL

HELMSMAN   the man who steers the ship at sea.

HOLD   a large compartment below decks for the stowage of cargo and provisions.

HULL   the main body of a ship apart from all masts, rigging, engines, fittings, etc.

HURRICANE DECK   a platform, the breadth of the upper deck, fitted over the deckhouses of a passenger steamer, and used principally as a promenade.

JACK-YARD TOPSAIL   a triangular sail set above the mainsail in gaff-rigged vessels. The luff and foot of the sail are extended beyond the mast and gaff by jack-yards.

JACK-YARD TOPSAIL

JACK-YARD

GAFF

MAINSAIL

MAST

JIB   a triangular sail set before the foremast. Old sailing ships often carried as many as six jibs. Jibs are set on the stays; if there is more than one jib, the aftermost one is usually called a staysail. All triangular sails set from the stays of masts other than the foremast are known as staysails.

JIB-HEADED TOPSAIL   a triangular sail set above the mainsail in gaff-rigged vessels. Unlike the jack-yard topsail (see opposite), the jib-headed topsail just fills the area between mast and gaff.

KEEL   the lowest continuous member of a ship which forms its backbone and to which the stem, stern, and ribs of the frame of the hull are attached.

KETCH-RIGGED   a vessel rigged with two masts, a mainmast, and a mizzenmast, stepped before the steering wheel or rudder head.

MIZZENMAST   MAINMAST

WHEEL

KNOCKED-DOWN   originally refering to casks which had been taken apart by the cooper on board, the term now applies to sailing vessels rolled over by the wind or heavy seas so that the masts are in the water.

KNOT   the nautical measure of speed: one nautical mile (6,080 ft (1,853.19 m)) per hour. The term comes from the number of knots on the ship's log-line which ran out when the line was thrown overboard while a 28-second sandglass emptied itself. The knots were tied every 47ft 3in (15m) and gave the speed of the ship in nautical miles per hour. The term is always x knots, never x knots an hour.

LATEEN MIZZEN   a mizzen mast having a lateen sail (or a lateen sail used as a mizzen).

LATEEN-RIGGED   a vessel rigged with lateen sails.

LATEEN SAIL   a triangular sail set on a yard hung at about a 45° angle from the mast.

LEEBOARD   a heavy board hung over the side of a shallow-draught vessel and lowered into the water to prevent the vessel from making leeway - being blown sideways.

LEG-OF-MUTTON SAIL   a triangular mainsail used on small boats, hoisted from the top.

LOOSE-FOOTED   a fore-and-aft sail with no boom, or not laced to a boom.

BOOM

MAINSAIL LACED TO BOOM

BOOM

NO BOOM

LOOSE-FOOTED MAINSAIL

LOWER MAINMAST — the lowest part of the mainmast.

(MAIN TOPGALLANT) MAST

(MAIN TOPMAST)

LOWER MAINMAST

MIZZENMAST *

FOREMAST *

* THE VARIOUS SECTIONS OF THESE MASTS ARE NAMED SIMILARLY TO THOSE OF THE MAINMAST

LUFF — the leading edge of a fore-and-aft sail.

(HEAD)

(LEECH)

(FOOT)

LUFF

LUFF

LUG-RIGGED — a vessel rigged with one or more lugsails.

LUGSAIL   a four-sided fore-and-aft sail that hangs from a lug or gaff which is generally two-thirds the length of the foot, and which projects past the mast from which it is hoisted.

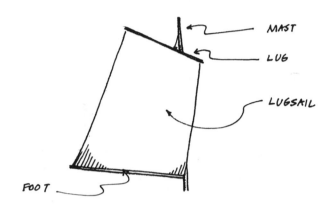

LUGSAIL-RIGGED   a vessel rigged with one or more lugsails.

LUG TOPSAIL   a topsail, with four sides, laced to a lug.

LUTCHET a form of mast housing on deck which allows the mast to be lowered when passing under low bridges. The mast is pivoted at the base rather than at the top of the fitting (as is the case with the tabernacle) and consequently only the back of the fitting is open.

LUTCHET   TABERNACLE

MAIN DECK the principal deck in a ship; in two-deck ships, the upper one; in ships with more than two decks, the second one down.

MAIN LUG the principal sail in a ship being a lugsail.

MAINMAST the largest mast on a ship.

MAINSAIL the principal sail of a sailing vessel. On a square-rigged ship the mainsail (usually called the main course) is the lowest (and largest) sail on the mainmast.

MAIN SQUARESAIL   a four-sided sail set on the main-mast.

MAIN TOPMAST   the middle section of a three-part mainmast.

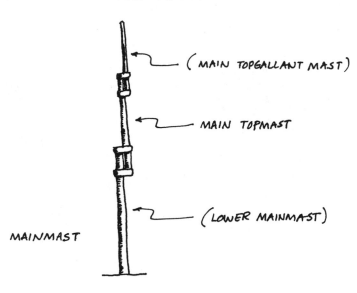

(MAIN TOPGALLANT MAST)

MAIN TOPMAST

(LOWER MAINMAST)

MAINMAST

MAIN YARD   the yard on the mainmast; if there be more than one such yard, the one from which the mainsail is hung.

MAINMAST

MAIN YARD

MAINSAIL

MAKE, TO — the way of expressing a ship's speed : she makes six knots, i.e. the ship moves at six nautical miles per hour.

MAST — a vertical spar (set in a ship) whose prime purpose is to carry sails, but which may also serve to carry wireless aerials and radar equipment.

MIDSHIPS — the central fore-and-aft line of a vessel. Also the waist, or middle of the fore-and-aft length.

MIZZEN — the name of the aftermost mast of a three- or more masted square-rigged sailing ship, and also the name of the small after-mast of a ketch or yawl.

MIZZEN LUG — a mizzen rigged with a lugsail.

MIZZENMAST — the mast from which the mizzen sail is set.

MIZZEN SAIL — the sail that is set from the mizzenmast.

MIZZEN TOPSAIL — the topsail set from the mizzenmast.

MIZZEN

MIZZEN TOPSAIL (FURLED)

MIZZEN
MIZZEN SAIL

SHIP

KETCH

423

NET BOAT — a fishing boat which fishes with nets rather than with hooked lines.

OAR — a wooden instrument which, used as a lever (the point of leverage being a fixture in the gunwale of the boat), pulls the boat through the water.

OAR OUTRIGGER — a framework extension to the sides of a hull designed to hold the oars, as of a galley.

OCTANT — a reflecting navigational instrument for measuring the altitude of heavenly bodies. It is called an octant because it has an arc of one eighth of a circle. The octant invented by John Hadley is shown on page 18.

ONE-MASTED   a vessel having one mast.

OUTBOARD   on the seaward side of the hull, such as an outboard engine which is generally placed aft the stern.

OUTRIGGER   a counterpoising log of wood rigged out from the side of a hull to provide additional stability; by extension, the vessel which has such an outrigger.

OVERALL LENGTH   the distance from the foremost part of the stem to the aftermost part of the stern. Often abbreviated to LOA.

PARROT BEAK   a distinctive form of prow, as shown.

PEAK   the upper, after corner of a four-sided fore-and-aft sail.

POLE MAST   a mast made from a single spar rather than several sections. This was the kind of mast used on polacres.

POOP   the name given to the short, aftermost deck raised above the quarterdeck of a ship, which in large ships comprised the roof of the captain's cabin.

PORT   the name given to the left-hand side of a vessel as viewed from aft.

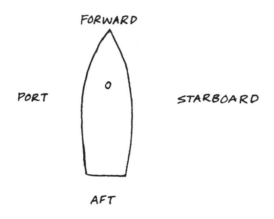

PORTHOLE   a corruption of the term "port," which was a square opening in the side of ships, for guns etc., and now often wrongly used to describe the round, glazed openings in the sides of modern ships, properly called scuttles.

PORT IN THE SIDE OF A WARSHIP

SCUTTLES IN A MODERN LINER

PRESS GANG the name given to those seamen whose job it was to bring in seamen for service in time of war, under the system known as impressment.

PROW a word used (rarely by sailors) to describe the forward end of a vessel.

QUARTER the after side of a ship.

QUARTER DECK that part of the upper deck abaft the mainmast (or where the mainmast would be), commonly reserved for the captain and officers.

RAFFEE TOPSAIL a triangular sail hung from the top of the mast to the yard below.

RAKE   the angle of the masts to the perpendicular.

MASTS RAKING AFT   NO RAKE

RAM   a projection from the bow of a warship, at or below the waterline, designed to sink an enemy ship by ramming.

RAM

RIG   the term used to describe the particular arrangement of masts and sails in a vessel.

RIG, TO   the operation, in a sailing vessel, of setting up the rigging and yards to receive the sails.

RIGGING   the term used to describe all lines, ropes, cables, and chains, which support the masts and spars, and which hoist, lower, and trim the sails.

ROUND-ENDED   a vessel with a rounded stern.

ROUND-STERNED   a vessel with a rounded stern.

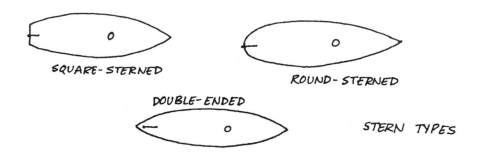

SQUARE-STERNED   ROUND-STERNED

DOUBLE-ENDED   STERN TYPES

RUDDER   a broad, flat device at the vessel's stern for steering.

STERN   TILLER

RUDDER   TILLER

RUDDER

DIRECTION BOAT MOVES

RUN BEFORE THE WIND, TO   blowing the vessel ahead.

the situation of a sailing vessel when the wind is

WIND

SAILS

RUNNING TACKLE   a pair of blocks connected by rope, which multiplies the power exerted on the rope, used for most lifting and moving jobs in a vessel.

BLOCK   LINE (ROPE)

STANDING END (FIXED)

RUNNING END (FREE)

TACKLE (PRONOUNCED TAYKAL)
ROVE* TO ADVANTAGE   * CONNECTED

SAIL   an assemblage of cloth designed to catch the wind and use its force to move a sailing vessel.

SAIL CLOSE TO THE WIND, TO   to point a sailing vessel as close into the wind as is possible and still achieve forward motion.

WIND

SALVAGE   a proportion of the value of a ship and her cargo paid to the rescuers who save her from danger. No salvage can be paid to the ship's own crew, however.

SCREW — the rotating propeller of a steamship, by which she is forced through the water.

SIDE VIEW   END VIEW

SCULL, TO — a method of propelling a boat forward by working an oar over the stern.

SET, TO — to fix the sails on a ship.

SETTEE SAIL — a four-sided Lateen sail (lateen sails having only three sides).

LATEEN SAIL   SETTEE SAIL

SHALLOW-DRAUGHT — a vessel drawing little water.

SHALLOW DRAUGHT   DEEP DRAUGHT   DRAUGHT

SHARP-ENDED   a vessel whose stern ends in a point.

SHEER   the curve fore-and-aft of the deck.

NO SHEER   VESSEL WITH SHEER

SHIP RIG, SHIP-RIGGED   a vessel with at least three square-rigged masts and a bowsprit.

SIDE DECK   a deck which runs only along the side of a vessel (as in a turret deck vessel) and does not extend the whole breadth of the vessel.

SPAR   a general term for any wooden support used in the rigging of a ship, such as masts, yards, booms, etc.

SPRITSAIL   a four-sided fore-and-aft sail the head of which is supported by a sprit, which extends upwards from the mast to the peak.

PEAK

HEAD

SPRIT

SPRITSAIL

SPRITSAIL - RIGGED   a vessel rigged with one or more spritsails.

SQUARE - ENDED   a vessel with a square stern; see the illustration on page 430.

SQUARE RIG   the arrangement of sails in a vessel where the sails are hung from yards which lie square to the mast.

SQUARE-RIGGED, SQUARE RIGGER   a vessel rigged with square sails hung from yards.

SQUARE SAIL   a four-sided sail hung from a yard set square to the mast

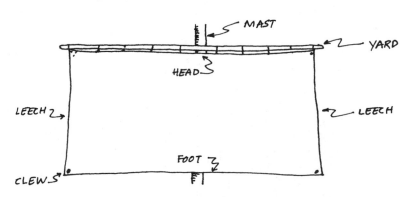

SQUARE-STERNED   a vessel having a square stern.

SQUARE-TOPSAIL   a four-sided topsail hung from a yard.

STANDING LUG MAINSAIL   a lugsail set on the mainmast with the forward end of the lug made fast to the mast, of which it then becomes a virtual extension.

STARBOARD   the right hand side of the vessel looking forward, so called from the early practice of hanging the steering oar or board from this side.

STAYSAIL   a sail set from a stay - a line supporting a mast.

STEEVE   the angle of the bowsprit in relation to the horizontal.

STEM   the foremost member of the bow of a vessel, which joins the keel.

STEMHEAD   the top of the stem.

STEP, TO   the operation of erecting a mast.

STERN   the after end of a vessel.

STERNCASTLE   the structure built in the stern of medieval ships, from which the archers and soldiers fought.

STERNPOST   the aftermost member in a vessel's framework which joins the keel. See illustration at top of page.

STERN-TO   to proceed stern first.

SWEEP   a very long, heavy oar carried on sailing vessels for use when the wind failed.

TABERNACLE a fitting on deck in which the bottom of the mast is hinged, allowing it to be lowered when passing under bridges. See illustration on page 421.

TACK the lower, forward corner of a fore-and-aft sail.

TAFFRAIL the after rail at the stern of a ship. Also in modern usage the aftermost deck area.

THREE-MASTED, THREE MASTER a sailing vessel having three masts.

THWART a transverse wooden seat in a small boat, such as the seat in a rowboat on which the oarsman sits.

TILLER — the wooden or metal bar that controls the rudder.

TOPGALLANT MAINMAST — the third section of the mainmast.

TOP MAINMAST — the second section of the mainmast

TOPMAST — the second section of a complete mast.

PARTS OF A COMPLETE MAST

TOPPING LIFT — a line which hoists or lowers the end of a spar.

TOPSAIL   the sail set next above the mainsail. In many square-rigged ships the topsail became two sails: upper and lower-topsail.

TOTAL DISPLACEMENT   the weight of the water which a ship displaces when floating fully loaded. This, at the rate of .35 cubic feet per ton (.9 cubic meters per .8 metric tons) is the actual weight of the ship, since a floating body displaces its own weight in water.

TRANSOM   the transverse timbers, which, fixed to the sternpost, give a vessel a flat stern.

TRANSOM STERN   a vessel whose stern is constructed as a transom.

TRIM, TO   the act of adjusting the weight in a vessel so that she floats at the required angle, and the act of adjusting the sails so that they lie at the best angle to the wind.

TRUCK   the fitting at the top of a mast through which various lines pass.

TWO-BERTH   a vessel with sleeping accommodations for two people.

TWO-MASTED, TWO MASTER   a vessel having two masts.

439

UNSHIP, TO   to detach or remove something from its fixed position, such as oars and masts.

UPPER DECK   the highest of those decks which run the full length of the ship. In those ships that have more than one deck it is the deck above the main deck.

WAIST   that part of the upper deck which lies between the forecastle and the quarter deck, or between the fore- and mainmasts.

WASHBOARD, WASHSTRAKE   a movable upper strake or board which may be attached to the gunwales of some open boats to keep out water.

WATERLINE LENGTH   the length, from bow to stern, of a vessel at the waterline.

WHEEL   the steering wheel, which is attached to the rudder.

WHEELHOUSE the deckhouse which houses the steering wheel. In large ships it is part of the bridge.

WINDWARD the side from which the wind blows.

YARD a large wooden or metal spar which crosses a mast and from which sails are hung. In square-riggers the yard is horizontal, in lateen-rigged vessels the yard crosses the mast diagonally.

SQUARE YARD   LATEEN YARD

YARD TOPSAIL a topsail which is set from a yard.

YAWL-RIGGED a vessel having two masts, a mainmast and a small mizzenmast stepped aft of the steering gear.

Bibliography

There are so many books on nautical matters that a complete bibliography of the subject would fill many, many pages. This, therefore, is a small, select list of books which are among my favorites, and which I think would appeal to readers of this book.

ANDERSON, ROMOLA, and R.C., THE SAILING SHIP: SIX THOUSAND YEARS OF HISTORY. New York: W.W. Norton & Company, Inc., 1963
A small classic, tracing the whole known history of ships.

BLOOMSTER, EDGAR L., SAILING AND SMALL CRAFT DOWN THE AGES. Annapolis, Maryland: The United States Naval Institute, 1940
A good reference book of sailing vessels in encyclopedic form.

BUDD, RHONDA, ed., SAILING BOATS OF THE WORLD: A GUIDE TO CLASSES. Englewood Cliffs, New Jersey: Prentice Hall, Inc., 1974
A very complete book of specifications and illustrations of practically all contemporary small boat classes.

CHAPELLE, HOWARD I., AMERICAN SMALL SAILING CRAFT: THEIR DESIGN, DEVELOPMENT AND CONSTRUCTION. New York: W.W. Norton & Company, Inc., 1951
Howard I. Chapelle is a noted marine author who has written several excellent books on ships and boats, most of them now standard works.

443

BIBLIOGRAPHY

CHAPMAN, CHARLES F.,   PILOTING, SEAMANSHIP AND SMALL BOAT HANDLING.   New York: The Hearst Corporation, 1963
    This is the standard book for anyone who would have anything to do with small boats in America.

HEATON, PETER,   SAILING. Harmondsworth, Middlesex, England: Penguin Books Ltd., 1949
    The first book I ever read on sailing and still my favorite.

KEMP, PETER, ed.,   THE OXFORD COMPANION TO SHIPS AND THE SEA.   London: Oxford University Press, 1976
    A wonderfully compendious book covering almost everything.

LANDSTRÖM, BJÖRN,   THE SHIP.   New York: Doubleday & Company, Inc., 1961
    A copious and well-illustrated history of ships.

LETHBRIDGE, T.C.,   COASTWISE CRAFT.   London: Methuen & Co. Ltd., 1952
    A small but charming book about English coastal craft.

PAASCH, H.,   ILLUSTRATED MARINE ENCYCLOPEDIA. Antwerp, 1890
    Although very old, still the best dictionary of ships and their parts ever produced.

ROSS, WALLACE,   SAIL POWER.   New York: Alfred A. Knopf, Inc., 1973
    As its subtitle states, this is "the complete guide to sails and sail handling."

TRE TRYCKARE, CAGNER & CO., designers,   THE LORE OF SHIPS. Gothenburg, Sweden: Tre Tryckare Ab, 1963
    A large book of illustrations, from various sources, of all sorts of things nautical.

WARD, RALPH T.,   SHIPS THROUGH HISTORY. Indianapolis and New York: The Bobbs-Merrill Company, Inc., 1973
    A very readable introduction to the subject.

444

Index

OF NAMED VESSELS

H.M.S. means the vessel belongs to the Royal Navy
H.M.Y. means the vessel belongs to the British Crown
U.S.S. means the vessels belongs to the United States Navy

Finis